WHEN I CROSSED NO-BOB

WHEN I CROSSED NO-BOB

BY

MARGARET McMULLAN

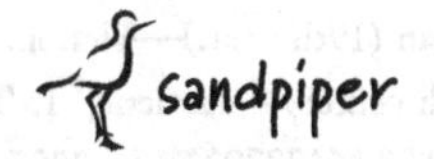

HOUGHTON MIFFLIN HARCOURT
BOSTON NEW YORK

www.sandpiperbooks.com

The text of this book is set in 11.5-point Bulmer.

The Library of Congress has cataloged the hardcover edition as follows:

McMullan, Margaret.
When I crossed No-Bob / by Margaret McMullan.
p. cm.
Summary: Ten years after the Civil War's end, twelve-year-old Addy, abandoned by her parents, is taken from the horrid town of No-Bob by schoolteacher Frank Russell and his bride, but when her father returns to claim her she must find another way to leave her O'Donnell past behind.

[1. Farm life—Mississippi—Fiction. 2. Abandoned children—Fiction. 3. Race relations—Fiction. 4. Reconstruction (U.S. history, 1865–1877) —Fiction. 5. Ku Klux Klan (19th cent.)—Fiction. 6. Mississippi—History —19th century—Fiction.] I. Title.
PZ7.M4787923Whe 2007
[Fic]—dc22
2007012753
ISBN: 978-0-618-71715-6
ISBN: 978-0-547-23763-3 pb

Manufactured in the United States of America
DOH 10 9 8 7 6 5 4 3
4500386836

For my mother, Madeleine

&

For my niece and godchild, Madeleine

Chapter 1

Some folks say if you marry wearing a brown dress, you'll live in the country, so I guess this new bride I see in front of us will live in town even though we don't have a town anymore.

She's wearing a white dress Momma says is made of cashmere with a hoop skirt made out of grapevines and her name is Irene. The one-room schoolhouse folks also use for church is open, and Momma and I can see this Irene walking up the middle of the room with a big man.

Momma and I are the only O'Donnells around and she bends to whisper in my ear. "Addy O'Donnell, you mind me and stay close."

This Irene, she looks to be the kind of lady who grew up in one of those big two-story houses, with columns, and a separate kitchen and dining room built of logs set apart from the main house. While cooks kept busy all day cooking, this Irene, she probably had a slave fanning her to sleep. Before the war, that is. Back when they had slaves.

This big man is walking Irene to her beau, who is a tall man with sandy hair, and he looks happy-scared, his eyes crinkly from smiling. I know him to be the schoolteacher. His name is Mr. Frank Russell and both he and Miss Irene are lucky because they're getting married and they have all their teeth.

In the front-row pews I can see Mr. Frank's pa with one arm and Mr. Frank's ma who has both her arms—one of them around her little boy and the other around the flower girl who I know is called Little Bit.

"By golly, I wish that Irene'd marry me," says Mr. McCollum, standing outside near us, wearing his fancy pants that hang from his bony body.

Miss Irene's uncle gives her away because her pa died in the war. Her uncle must weigh as much as a good cow and I wonder how Mr. Frank, who looks to weigh not much over 120, summoned the courage to ask that big man for his only niece's hand in marriage. What gave him that kind of brave?

We all watch Miss Irene and Mr. Frank smiling with their teeth, their foreheads touching while Brother Davenport says words. They say their vows and when they kiss, I don't look away. I wonder if their love is fierce like Momma says her love for Pappy is. I wonder if Mr. Frank will ever go away to Texas like my pappy did.

When Pappy left, the misery attacked Momma and she turned into a different person. I know what to do when Momma has a cold or the stomach cramps. I fix her up with a nice cup of life-everlasting tea the way she taught me. And if the chills or fevers come, I dig up some horsemint to add to the tea. But I can't heal this hurt she's had since Pappy left us, and she hasn't even asked me to try. I wish for once she would just ask me.

Somebody somewhere inside is playing a sweet song on the harmonica.

Their neighbors come out happy and spread out the cloths to make for a fine feast. These ladies must have been making pound cakes for more than a week. Even though we were not invited and most likely should not be here, Momma and I pretend to be happy too, though it is not hard with all this food and happiness before us. Momma teaches me to do like her. We straighten our thin brown calico dresses and smile, both of us hoping for chicken and cake.

She bends down, spits on a rag, and rubs hard on the scar that runs down the side of my nose. Dirt always goes there first.

If you look closely, you can see that Momma was pretty once. Now, her face is sunken in and lined up with worry, sorrow, anger, and hunger. When Pappy left, her hair went from blond to brown to white all in one year, and her eyes are always puffy from crying.

I recognize most everybody from church. We O'Donnells all attend Sunday services. Around here, if you don't go to church, you're not a person at all, but an animal. Around here, if you don't go to church, the elders come and get you and make you go to church, and if you still don't go, you are shunned, which is worse than being an animal. The O'Donnells pride ourselves on going to church. The O'Donnell men stand their guns in the corner of the church during preaching. People have gotten used to us all coming in barefooted.

There is a pit dug out in the ground with Mr. Pig in there front and center, spinning and roasting, and chicken pies like

I've never seen. Everywhere I look, I see flowers and children playing at marbles, hopscotch, run-and-catch, climbing trees, gathering nuts. Ard Reacy is playing "Turkey in the Straw" on his fiddle, and after his dog, Old Shep, looks up from his sleep, he starts in on "Molly Put the Kettle On."

So many of the men have stumps for arms or cane legs made from timber. They sit on benches from the schoolhouse, split logs with pegs for legs, pegs just like the ones they wear. After the war was over, they all came crawling back to Smith County half-dead or half-alive.

When Pappy was here, he told me stories about the war and the world too.

After the war, after the gunfire and the cannons and the fires, O'Donnells and Smith County folks both, soldiers and deserters, straggled back all ragtag after fighting at Second Manassas, Antietam, Fredericksburg, Chancellorsville, Gettysburg, and others. They all came back with the guns they kept even though they were supposed to give them up and promise never ever to take up arms against the government of the United States again. After the war almost every family was armed.

After the North burned our country and moved on, the Yankees put the state under martial law and had an army of colored soldiers stationed in Jackson. Their watchword was "White man, bottom rail's on top now."

So here we are, ten years later in this time called peace, when folks still sometimes walk around like they are sleeping, half clothed, half fed, one ear or both still ringing from the four years of war noise.

Pappy said after the war, the light was different. Most all of the trees were gone from fire or used for lumber and there was hardly any shade to be had. It turned hotter in the summer, colder in the winter. After the war, Pappy said we were all worse off.

Ard Reacy fiddles out "Dixie" and someone yells for him to quit, then someone else says no, go on. The wedding party falls silent and we all listen to Ard while we think on what all we've lost.

Every morning we still wake up and see nothing but ruins—ruined towns, ruined railroads, ruined trees, ruined houses. Where there was once a house, maybe there's a chimney or some steps leading to nowhere. You get to feeling ruined yourself. Hollow. With nobody coming to help. Nobody from the North. You look up at the sky and wonder if someone or something is going to just plop down and give a hand. Some cornmeal would be a mighty sight. And you know by the time anybody or anything comes, you'll be too angry to say thank you. This hollow feeling is worse than mad. It's a no-feeling that doesn't feel human-like.

After the war, after the Yankees came and left, Pappy said they took all our horses and mules and killed all our cows and chickens and pigs. They didn't leave us nothing to eat and we're likely to starve to death. Everybody in these parts was mad and hungry and armed. Momma and me, we still use parched potato peels to make coffee, and every day I dig up the dirt in the smokehouse, drip that through the hopper, then boil it to get the salt. We're lucky, though. Least we're not eating dirt and green corn like I seen Walt O'Donnell's children do.

Ard Reacy finishes playing "Dixie" and a few people clap.

Some of the people look our way and I steady myself for the mumbling. Some folks even back away. I know what they see: *These here are beggars and they are white!* Some might not even see our skin on account of some of the dirt I missed. Are they backing away because they are afraid of me, a twelve-year-old half their size? We know what they *say* about us. They say the O'Donnells is no better than termites. We only do harm and you can't get rid of us.

It's true what they say about the O'Donnells harnessing

people instead of mules in No-Bob. Pappy and Anse plowed their own brother Garner and at noon put him in a mule stall and fed him hay and corn. Of course, he didn't eat, but I guess if they'd have told him to, he would have tried.

That's just the O'Donnell way.

Nona Dewitt prances my way and says, "Why don't you find your brother or your pa and marry him. That's what all you people do."

"I don't got no brother and my pappy's gone."

"Hush," Momma says. Nona Dewitt and her followers laugh because I don't get whatever joke Nona has just told.

"Stand up proud," Momma says. "You're an O'Donnell."

These people here at the wedding never walk the plank that crosses the stream into No-Bob because they figure like Bob, they won't come out.

Momma told me the story about how No-Bob got its name. One day, after the war, a freed black man named Bob, looking for some land to stake a claim, took a wrong turn and wandered into O'Donnell territory. The O'Donnells banded together. To take the colored situation in hand, they said. Bob never left. To set an example for Yankee justice, the sheriff in Smith County sent out a search party. People were everywhere looking, but they couldn't find Bob. They were so tired and distraught when they came out of the hollow, they just said, "No Bob," and that's what the people of Smith County have called the place ever since. No-Bob.

Pappy liked that people were fearful of him and all the other O'Donnells. "We have a history," he used to say. I puff out my chest and try on some of that O'Donnell scare. I try it on to make myself feel better around the likes of Nona Dewitt.

I can see that Momma is listening to the talk about the newlyweds. They got some land and a dwelling house. She tells me to pay attention and listen for silver in people's purses and pockets and point those people out to her.

Momma is talking to a man with a mule and a wagon. I hear her, but I'm not listening. I'm still looking at all the food, wondering, *When do we eat?* I pull on Momma's dress.

"Leave us alone now," the man says to me.

"You heard him," Momma says. "Now go on."

Momma is telling the man with the mule her burdens and sorrows I've heard her tell people before. She says the word "Texas," and when the man starts to nod, I have to turn away.

After Pappy got into a brawl with Garner O'Donnell, the brother he plowed, Garner shot Pappy in the arm. Pappy stood awhile, bleeding in front of Garner, saying how dare he shoot him with little itty-bitty buckshot. It was an insult. Momma sewed Pappy up and declared him leadproof.

That's when Pappy left us for Texas. He said he would send for us when he could, but that was so many years ago, I can hardly remember his face.

Some folks say after being in the war for so long, Pappy got to missing the war and all the roaming around and all the bloody battles.

Momma looks away from the man with the mule toward me. She looks at me differently, like I'm a sack of bricks she's tired of hauling.

I sneak food and eat under a clump of trees. People notice and pretend not to see or not to mind.

The girl they call Little Bit is not so little. She's tall and blond like her mother and I catch her peachy smell as she passes. I tell her hey. She asks me my name and I tell her.

"Addy O'Donnell," I say. "I'm twelve."

She tells me she's thirteen.

"I know a trick," she says, and she makes the exact same sound as a crow.

"How you do that?"

"My big brother Frank taught me. He can teach anything. You want a cake?" She gives me one. We go and eat cakes standing down near the creek people say runs into the Tallahala. It's the same creek that divides No-Bob and the rest of Smith County. Across the creek, we see two Choctaw women cutting cane to use to make their baskets. They are quiet and even though me and Little Bit watch, they don't look over at us.

They are what they were before the war, ever since they gave up their land at the Treaty of Dancing Rabbit Creek, when Mississippians took away their homes. They're not slaves, not landowners, not white, not black. They're squatters.

One of the Choctaw women looks up at me, and for a minute, it feels like we recognize each other.

Little Bit's talking about all the land her pa and her brother have just bought, most of it Indian land, and she's all smug in her pink and white dress and ribbons. She talks more than plenty. In the water, our faces are side by side, same size but nothing alike. She's light-skinned and light-haired; I'm ruddy-skinned with dull hair and dark eyes that people say make me look devilish. I am dirty, it's true, and Little Bit has shoes and I do not.

"My ma was baptized in the Tangipahoa River in Magnolia," she says. "I was baptized here. Where were you baptized?"

I don't say nothing.

"What happened to your nose?" Little Bit asks me. "How did you get that scar?"

I don't want to tell this pretty little girl that I haven't been baptized yet and that my pappy swiped me with a poplar stick because I was up to no good, not after she told me what her big brother can teach her.

"I'm from a family," I say right proud. "About the meanest family there ever was."

I don't know what gets into me. Momma always says it's the devilment I get from Pappy, but I take to splashing Little Bit a little bit, and then a lot. She tells me to quit it and I don't. And all of a sudden, she's mad and I'm mad, and we're on the banks and we're down in it, fighting, and I'm painting that clean little pink face with mud and this Little Bit? She's no little chip. She's scratching and punching and we go at it, and all the while I'm thinking, *This here wedding is big fun—just like an O'Donnell wedding.*

But then they come screaming. They all do. The whole wedding party comes running down to the creek, screaming all at once. They don't mumble but say outright that I'm bad

bad bad. Evil. Painting a white girl black like that, and then trying to drown her. Little Bit cries to hear them and her mother holds her tight.

In all the fuss, I can't find Momma.

Only the menfolk hold me by the arms. No one else will touch me. They don't want to get themselves dirty. I lean this way and that, trying to find the man with the mule. Maybe he knows where Momma is.

"Someone get this girl's momma," Mr. Frank Russell says.

Everyone nods, mumbling yes, that's what should be done. A few women take their sons and daughters aside, like they don't want their children to see the likes of me. They head out to help pack away the food and fold the linens.

Nobody seems to know where my momma is.

I am the last one at the wedding picnic and nobody knows what to do with me. I'm old enough to set out on my own, so that is just what I do. I start out alone on the road. People loading up their wagons, looking at me passing, shake their heads. Brother Davenport is talking with Mr. Frank when Miss Irene, the newlywed bride, stops me and takes my hand. She tells her new husband they'll take me home. She says she knows where I live.

I can see that it angers and pleases Mr. Frank at once. He looks at me and frowns, and then looks at his new wife, who is smiling a soft, lippy smile that makes me ashamed of myself and the way I look. He hitches up his wagon to his mule and we three climb in, ready to go to No-Bob.

Chapter 2

After the brightness of the wedding, all I see around me is the gray gray grayness that is No-Bob, as though while we were gone all the color ran out of the land. Nobody's at my house in No-Bob. No Momma, nobody. The sky is white. Mr. Frank and Miss Irene don't know I can read the GONE TO TEXAS sign on the door. And I know it to be true.

We step over the circle of eggshells. Neither Mr. Frank nor Miss Irene asks and I don't explain. If you are ever anxious for your sweetheart to come back from a trip, Momma says to put a pin in the ground with the point up and then put an egg on the point. When the insides run out of the egg, your sweetheart will return. The empty shells circle our house. Never mind that we could have eaten those eggs.

Momma went off with the man with the mule to find Pappy and to be free of me. She told me herself she had a fierce love, a fierce love for Pappy but not for me. I look at all the eggshells around our house, and I know she is gone, I know this to be true all at once, and it makes me feel as blank as the sky.

Mr. Frank leans into his new wife's side, and I think that he must be smelling her yellow hair while he whispers some of the things I hear. I hear: "The O'Donnells are trouble." I hear: "self-willed" and "haughty." I hear something about discipline.

"We've never had a speck of trouble from the O'Donnells, Frank."

Mr. Frank says louder, "I don't care, Irene. We can find some of her people. They'll have to take her in. Anyplace but ours." I hear Mr. Frank say some other words I've never heard. Miss Irene shushes him, and then I hear him say "filthy."

Least he doesn't say I'm ugly.

Miss Irene, she says there are some things she can fix, and even though I can't see her face, I can tell from the sound of her words that she's smiling sweet.

Mr. Frank sets his mule in motion, and the three of us are riding again, passing the oak where General Jackson is said to have hitched his horse while taking a rest off Jackson's Military Road.

As soon as we cross the stream and head out of No-Bob, we pass the two Indian women Little Bit and I saw down at the creek. They are walking single file on their way to the Cohay bottoms where they will probably camp and make more swamp cane baskets to trade.

I am a squatter like the Indians. I should go with them and make camp too. But no, if I go down to the river and camp like an Indian, Momma will not find me when she comes back to get me.

Queen Anne's lace waves at us, lining the dirt road out of town, our passing wagon raising red dust. I wonder which flower or herb would make a good healing tea for the hurt I'm feeling now.

Mr. Frank's dwelling house is all log, and he even thought to build it up off the ground away from dirt, bugs, and termites. The corncribs and the smokehouse are built with logs too, but they are built right on top of the ground. There are stalls too, though there is no horse or plow in sight. They've already had a barn raising and someone thought to plant a grove of young pecan trees out front, which will make for good shade when they mature.

Wooden steps lead us up to a front porch where two piles of firewood are stacked high up to the roof. Inside they have a fireplace made out of rocks with big hooks fastened into the side to swing pots round on. Meal and flour barrels set in one corner of the kitchen, and an old muzzle-loading shotgun leans up in another corner, near a spinning wheel, the shuttle to the loom, and a closet built with lock and key. Pegs driven between the logs in the wall hold saddlebags, shot pouches, and a holster. The floor is not bare earth, but laid logs split into planks. I can smell the newness of the pine wood. There are chairs around a table and a setback for all the dishes.

Miss Irene takes my hand gently and tells me Mr. Frank carved the closet doors. All their doors close with wooden latches. That Mr. Frank, he went all out and bought seven panes of glass for all seven of his windows. And now he has glass windows such as I've never seen. It looks to me that Mr. Frank built his house to last a good long while.

Miss Irene has already come and decorated the walls with pictures of flowers and baskets of fruit, but I don't understand why she would want a picture of a dead fish hanging in her front room.

Mr. Frank hauls in a mattress from the barn and sets it near the fireplace.

"You'll stay here the night," he says. "We'll see about tomorrow."

Miss Irene fixes up the mattress with a sheet and a quilt. "Perhaps your mother will come tomorrow," she says. "Sweet dreams, Addy."

Lying down on the mattress, I listen to them talk, late into the night. I hear Mr. Frank saying "Garner O'Donnell." Garner is my uncle, the one who shot Pappy. I hear Mr. Frank tell his new wife that Garner tried to cheat him out of his own land. Mr. Frank says that even though the judge in Raleigh ruled for Mr. Frank, he's still sore at that Garner and all the other O'Donnells.

"Mean makes mean and more mean," I hear Mr. Frank say.

"Oh, Frank," Miss Irene says. "That was one man. You can't blame them all for what one did."

I listen to Mr. Frank's voice and it sounds like he still has some of what Pappy used to call "grudge business" to take care of with Garner and maybe even with all the other O'Donnells.

"The O'Donnells are trouble, Irene. She'll only bring harm."

My toes touch the smooth surface of warm stones at the foot of the mattress and I breathe in the smell of pine needles and dried moss it's stuffed with. Miss Irene boiled rocks and put some under the quilt to keep my feet warm. Even though it is not cold, I can't stop shivering.

I wonder if I should stick a pin in an egg for Momma. I know about hoping and praying for something, and I've heard prayers myself when I've paid attention in church, but I still don't know the words. So I lay there in the dark, tapping my toenails against the rocks, saying my own words of prayer.

"Monday, Tuesday, Wednesday, Thursday," I whisper. "Friday, Saturday, Sunday." I say that over and over.

This is the farthest I've ever been from home.

Already, I have forgiven Momma. At least she didn't send me to the orphans' home in Jackson. These here are hard times. Not but a month ago Hazel O'Donnell sent her two girls, Mattie Lou and Dora, off down the road to fend for themselves. They were fourteen and fifteen, both not much older than me.

It's a shame I'm making so much trouble, and this on their wedding night. I could climb out the window right now and leave. I'm not scared either. I remember my momma talking to that man with the mule. I hope he is a nice man. I hope he takes good care of her until she finds Pappy. "Now go on." That's what she said to me.

I hook my thumbs in the armpits of my too-tight cast-off dress from a cousin whose momma said she'd never take in a child from my momma. I don't know why the O'Donnells didn't like Momma. A castoff. That's who *she* was and that's what I am now. I should leave, I should. I don't got no momma, no pappy, and no home. I might as well be dead.

The rocks heat up my feet plenty so I can start to sleep. It's a long time, but just feeling the rocks with my toes and thinking about Miss Irene being so nice makes me feel good enough to sleep.

I get up before the sun, bring in some wood from the front porch, and build a fire. Mr. Frank and Miss Irene have a good new log house, but not much else. There sits a three-legged skillet over hot coals, so, remembering how Momma used to make me and Pappy johnnycakes, I get together a poke of cornmeal, mix it with some cold water, put it on a clapboard, and set it near the hot coals. Momma complained about my cooking, but she never complained that I cooked. I eat one piece of bread to show Mr. Frank I won't take up too much room or food.

If Momma was here, she'd be going through their house. She'd see what she could find of theirs to make her own. But I shake Momma thoughts out of my head and look outside the window.

Mr. Frank is smart. I can see he is already outside working, digging up the ground himself with a grubbing hoe, laying in crops, growing them something to eat.

Nobody has to show me to work. Like most folks, they have a smokehouse in the backyard, an outhouse, a barn, a pen for their one hog, and the pasture way out back. Out past the pasture are the woods, the longleaf pines taller than anything else around. The outhouse is near the hog pen, which I think is smart—it's all just one big smell, in one place, unless of course the wind changes direction.

I head out to the barn with a clean bucket. Someone must have given Mr. Frank and Miss Irene a cow for their wedding, so I milk this cow, run my hands over her back, and pet her until her eyes close and I know she wants to be left alone. I toss hay to the mule and clean out her stall. I pet her hair and nuzzle with her. I want to get up on her back and lay there for a while, but instead, I get corn from the corncrib and feed the chickens. I don't see any eggs so I crouch down to the chickens and say hey, thinking that might make them give me an egg.

Miss Irene keeps her water bucket on the back porch, not the front porch, and I bring in a bucket of fresh water, knowing they'll want coffee.

They have a nice well dug deep in their front yard. They don't have a springhouse and I think to lower the milk into the well wall to keep it cool and fresh. The wind blows and the mouth of the well plays music. I hum along.

Inside Miss Irene is grinding coffee for a fresh pot and she is a might pleased with my johnnycakes. She struggles with the weight of the water bucket, slopping the water, trying to pour it into the kettle to boil. I say, "How 'bout we make the water my job?"

Mr. Frank comes in smiling, looking at his Irene.

"Look at what Addy made us for breakfast, Frank."

It's like Mr. Frank forgot I was there and his smile disappears. He eats fast and heads outside again. He's got corn and cotton planted and I can see his eyes making plans for more. His land has a big reed brake and he's opened up a nice farm on this tract. This Mr. Frank, he knows about land and how to make it make food and maybe even a little money.

I fill the wood box in the kitchen with wood and tote out the ashes. Near about midmorning when I come back in, Miss Irene stands over the kettle stirring up black smoke from something burned and terrible-smelling.

"Mr. Frank's ma and pa are coming," she says. "Can you cook?" Miss Irene is nice and soft but she cannot cook.

At noon Mr. Frank's ma and pa arrive with jars of pickled peaches, stewed tomatoes, and Little Bit and her little brother, little Jack.

Little Bit is all pigtails and giggles and she jumps off the back of the wagon and hugs me like I'm her sister, like fighting the way we did yesterday is what we always do. A pecan-colored man named Sunny Rise and his son Jess Still Rise drive the wagon. They work for Mr. Frank's ma and pa. Miss Irene gives me two plates heaped full of food to give to the colored man and his son.

"Why they call you Jess Still?" I ask the little boy. His left eye stays fixed on me while his right eye checks out what else is going on.

"On account of I stands still all the times," the little boy says. His father laughs.

"He's a good boy," his pa says. I look at Jess Still and can't help but wish I could be so good without having to try so hard. While they pull the wagon around, I watch their backs lean in together and all of the sudden I miss my momma and pappy something terrible.

Miss Irene has spread out a nice table. She says she wants this to be an extra-special lunch because she feels bad that she took away their Frank. She says when Mr. Frank's pa and older brother left to join in the fighting, Mr. Frank got real close to his momma on account of all the time they spent together during the war years, and what with the grandpa leaving, and the grandma dying, and then the terrible news that his brother Henry was killed—well, it was hard, hard on everybody.

In no time flat Miss Irene learned me and Little Bit how to wait on the table. While they eat, Mr. Frank talks about all that he wants—a carriage for Irene, a grist on his property, and a sawmill too. Then they wouldn't have to keep going to the mill and gin near the Jones County line. They laugh to think of all this dreaming.

"Have you heard from Buck?" Mr. Frank asks his ma.

She shakes her head. "Not since he wrote to say he couldn't come for the wedding."

"Who's Buck?" I say.

They all look at me, remembering I'm still here.

"Buck was a slave," Little Bit says.

"And Buck was a friend," Mr. Frank corrects her. "He was like a brother to me."

Little Bit goes on like she's telling me some once-upon-a-time story. "Pa and Frank walked Buck to the river Strong. Pa give Buck a pair of eyeglasses and his freedom papers and then he crossed over."

"Pa *gave* Buck," Mr. Frank says.

"He's in New York City now," Little Bit goes on.

"They say that when a person crosses that river called Strong, the Lord gives you what you want," Mr. Frank's pa says. "When we were there, I told the Lord I don't want nothing much, only to get back home. And here we are."

Mr. Frank smiles and makes a toast to his pappy. I nod, wondering about this family. What crazy people set their slaves free before the fighting was over?

We eat the pickled peaches and I say to myself, *These here peaches are now my favorite food.*

I clear the table while Miss Irene and Mr. Frank's ma clean up in the kitchen. Miss Irene says she's sorry because she doesn't have enough sugar for the coffee. She sent me over before noon to borrow a cup from a neighbor, and the neighbor lady sent the sugar back with me with a note saying to pay back in full measure. Miss Irene sent me to take the sugar back.

"That woman will not lecture me on rules of conduct," Miss Irene says to Mr. Frank's ma, who has a nice, gentle laugh.

I serve the men their coffee on the porch and listen to their talk about Mr. Frank starting a general store. He's saying how hard it is for people in the county to get things. He says they have to drop everything just so they can go to New Orleans or Montgomery for three days when he could get a whole lot of things himself, bring it back, then sell it all off for a profit. It's such a fine idea, I can hardly believe someone else hasn't thought it up.

Mr. Frank's pa talks about a store that opened on the Taylorsville-Williamsburg road. The owner hung a coffeepot over his door and served coffee made with fresh spring water and beans from New Orleans, using molasses drippings to sweeten it. A person could get either long or short sweetening, but no cream.

"Well, there's no post office here that's accessible and folks like a place to sit and talk," Mr. Frank's pa says. He says he'll back him and they clink coffee cups to seal the deal.

Mr. Frank's pa leans on the porch pole, itching his stump while he looks me over. He moves slow. I know that he lost his arm in the war. Everyone has a story. But I'm not clear how the big story really started. All I know is that they were mad about something so they had a war.

"You could have this girl, Addy, do your work in a few years. Like Buck."

"She's not a slave, Pa."

I stand still while the two of them look me over.

"And she's not staying here forever."

As the day closes and Momma still doesn't come, I can see Mr. Frank making his surmising that Momma never did plan on coming back. If it were all up to him, I know he'd turn me loose. But he's aiming to please Miss Irene.

Momma knew what she was doing.

"Addy," he says after his pa, his ma, Little Bit, and Jack leave. "You don't need to be doing boys' work outside. Miss Irene will teach you to help out with the washing, ironing, baking, and the common et cetera of the house."

I know that Mr. Frank does not want me around him. Outside, he can be alone.

After he leaves the house, I have to ask Miss Irene if Mr. Frank always talks like a schoolteacher. "And who et Zet up?"

Miss Irene laughs, says for me to never mind, then shows me about rolling out dough because tomorrow it's baking day.

I miss Momma, but I am glad that Momma's misery weren't no catching sickness. Mr. Frank and Miss Irene have been nothing but good to me and this makes me feel growed up and good myself. They make me want to do right. I am not hungry either and I feel quicker and not so mad. I try to remember the word for what I am feeling. And then I recall. *Happy*. I am happy.

Chapter 3

From May to September I work hard to prove to Mr. Frank that me and all the other O'Donnells aren't the lazy, mean good-for-nothings he thinks we are. Already it is October, and after I gather and put up the corn, after I dig the sweet potatoes and Miss Irene and I can the tomatoes and okra, after we make the maypop jelly and wild plum wine, after Mr. Frank kills the hog and we salt the meat down in the smokehouse so it won't rot, and after I bury the squash in the hay, Mr. Frank pays the one-dollar school tuition so that I can go to school with him and I can hardly stand it, I'm so excited. School is my reward.

All the work wasn't all bad either. Working with Mr. Frank goes fast. I tell him about everything—Momma, Pappy, I tell him about living when I lived in No-Bob. He listens and listens, taking it all in. I prove to Mr. Frank that I am a better worker outside than in.

Momma told me whistling inside or outside the house was bad luck, but I want to whistle right here, right now, so I do and I am glad that I am still able. I walk with Mr. Frank the three miles to the schoolhouse carrying a lard pail with our lunches. Meat and biscuits and two cold baked sweet potatoes. There is a puddle just outside the schoolhouse, and before I step inside, I step into the puddle to get my feet good and clean.

Mr. Frank, he stands aside and watches.

The schoolhouse is a pine log cabin with a dirt floor and a stick-and-dirt chimney. We children sit on split logs with pegs for legs. I take the back seat near a redheaded boy named Rew Smith so I can rest my back against the wall. The girl next to me says it is a hard matter to learn much after walking three miles to get here and then have to sit on these seats. I say I am just glad to be here.

We spend the morning studying our McGuffey's Reader. Mr. Frank says I'm not so far behind as he would have thought. He doesn't keep one switch in the room, and if students spell a word wrong, he doesn't whip us.

I need me some friends and I set to work. At lunchtime, outside, I start walking funny the way Pappy taught me. Pappy was the funniest man in No-Bob. Everybody liked Pappy. He showed me how to act like I'm hurting myself without hurting myself. He showed me how to make folks laugh, and they do. Little Bit laughs and so does her brother Jack. Even that girl Nona Dewitt laughs.

But then I hear Rew Smith say, "I won't play with that little O'Donnell girl. My pa told me not to." I hear: "That Addy. She's got the devil in her."

For lunch we all sit on the ground to eat. Little Bit says to look out for wild hogs who sometimes come up out of the woods and grab our food. Mr. Frank passes around a bottle of milk with letters marked on the bottle. There are no cups and we are to drink to the next letter. When Little Bit passes me the bottle, I hold it up. I am to drink to the letter *M* and I do. I pass it to Rew.

"I'm not drinking after her," Rew Smith says. His hair is

the color of red apples and I'm wondering if being with it in the sun makes him hotter. This Rew seems to have the respect of the others, and I recognize it. He's mean the way an O'Donnell is mean. He looks at me and comes so close I think he will push me down. "She's gotta be part nigger. That's what my pa says." I look at him, ready to fight. But Mr. Frank rings the bell for us to come back inside the schoolhouse. We are to learn more spelling, and after that comes arithmetic.

It is a long first day.

In my second week of attending Mr. Frank's school, I decide to play teacher. Surely this will win me friends.

Mr. Frank's desk is supplied with drawers in which he stores his books and what he calls the other et ceteras of his profession. He has a pipe he smokes, and while everyone files in, I light Mr. Frank's pipe with a match I find in his drawer, and I take to puffing it before Mr. Frank comes into the room. Everyone laughs. Everyone, even the older ones. Then, from the back of the room, Little Bit shouts, "Hey, Addy. You're turning green." And I commence to getting sick all over Mr. Frank's desk, and when I look up, there he is, standing in the doorway, Mr. Frank watching, shaking his head.

* * *

That evening after supper Mr. Frank catches me crying with the chickens. We sit together on a log under a tree and I am nothing but ashamed. Mr. Frank, he smiles at me, and from where I sit I can see that one of his front teeth sticks out past his bottom lip just a tad. I have not seen this before and it makes me smile because now that I seen this I think that Mr. Frank looks to be about twelve years old. I think of what he must have been like when he was my age, a little boy messing around, him and his pa sitting around the family table all happy-like, his ma feeding them pickled peaches, but as soon as I start thinking on that, I stop.

"I wish I had Momma back." The sun is not down yet and the sky is pinkish.

"But she punished you so much, Addy. You told me so yourself."

I close my eyes, wishing away what I've said. I should not have talked about Momma while I worked alongside Mr. Frank. I should have stayed loyal to her. Already I have told Mr. Frank too much. I have told him about Momma's seasons of sickness. I have told him how she locked me up in the chifforobe.

I tell Mr. Frank that it wasn't so bad, being in the chifforobe. It smelled of pine, and if I moved Momma's two hanging dresses and the folded-up quilt, it was big enough to stand up in, and because it was an old chifforobe, there were cracks for air and plenty of turning-around room to change positions every once in a while. When Momma shut me up in the dark after I did something wrong, I had time to think. I rubbed my eyes with my knees to see the pictures behind my eyelids. I counted the stars inside my mind.

"With all due respect to your momma, Addy, that's no way to punish a child."

"I know. But she made me. She could do what she wanted with me."

"God made you too, Addy."

"Did God make you?"

"Yes, Addy, he did."

"So we're kin?"

"You could say that."

We're looking down at the bald ground where the chickens are scratching. I have these dark feelings and I wish it was spring again instead of fall. The best thing to do is do like Mr. Frank and Miss Irene. Grow up, get married, and try to make a home for yourself. But what if I have a fierce love and a fierce marriage like Momma and Pappy's? But who would ever marry me, anyway? An O'Donnell. A termite.

"I'm mad at God. I don't think I like him."

"Why not, Addy?"

"'Cause he makes some of us rich and some poor. Some O'Donnells, some not. Why can't he just make us all pretty and rich?"

"I don't know. Maybe you need to ask him yourself. Talk to him."

"Talk to him how? Once, I knew a prayer called the Lord's Prayer, but I forget all the words."

"Talk to him like you would your own pa or ma."

"I don't know. He don't seem to be like most folk."

Mr. Frank puts his arm around me and squeezes me to him tight, so tight I think I might cry. "Start with thanking him."

And before I can say, "For what?" Mr. Frank says, "You need a pair of shoes, Addy. I'll make you a pair myself. But for now, let's just sit here for a while."

He doesn't say anything. I watch the leaves fall. A ladybug sets to crawling on my leg. Sitting here with Mr. Frank feels the way I think holding hands with the Lord would feel. Good. Close. Like you know you're going to be OK because you're with someone. I imagine that's what being married feels like too. Being in love must feel like sitting on a log with someone special, someone a little like yourself.

Chapter 4

I don't seem able to sit still and do my reading and writing work like the others. Even at Mr. Frank's house, Miss Irene wants me to sit on the stool in front of the weaver and spin thread and run the loom and I hate hate hate it because I'm bad at both weaving and sitting still. Miss Irene says I won't get good at it unless I stay at it. She says that's what her mother did for her. She says her mother says a woman's worth is determined by her tiny, even rows of stitches. I let that sit for a minute. But then Miss Irene laughs and lets me go outside.

She says around her house, people ought to do what they're naturally good at.

I feed the chickens and collect their eggs, milk and feed the cow, and clear out the stalls every day. I feed the new hogs corn to keep them tame, and when the acorns fall I take the hogs to the woods and let them root around some. I know it's time to cut a good supply of firewood when I see the hogs raking and toting straw, a sure sign of a cold spell.

Mr. Frank, he got himself some good land here with plenty of nut-bearing trees: big-bud and scaly-bark hickories, black walnut, chestnut, beech, pecan, and chinquapin. I pick plums from under the trees too and tote them to the two hogs so they'll taste better. I gather red-oak, elm, maple, and juniper bark. I set it out to dry and then grind it up so we can stew it down and use it to dye. We use borax, alum, and bluestone to set the dye. I set aside some red-oak bark for fevers and colds. Lots of things you can do to get ready for colds, like collecting and drying mullein and horsemint for teas. Momma taught me about such things that Miss Irene isn't so keen on.

One afternoon, I am sweeping the yard with a brush broom when Little Bit stops by, picks up another of Miss Irene's brooms, and starts sweeping alongside me, humming some song.

"After this, you want to play marbles?"

"Don't you got chores?" I say. Little Bit is pretty and young, so she gets spoiled. She plays. I work.

"I climb trees," she says, moving a pigtail. "I'm not a Miss Priss."

Miss Irene hails us from the porch. She sweeps and tells me to go on off and play. She says I've already done a fine job.

Little Bit and me, we don't say much. We just are and we are that together. We already had our fight down near Clear Creek at her brother's wedding, so it's like we've gotten that out of the way, and it was a good fight, because we were equal and neither one of us won and the two of us, we know how strong and how weak the other is.

While we are out and about we pick and collect the last of the wild plums that grow along a ditch in the thickets. We can help Miss Irene make jelly and pies.

You work and you work and you work and you eat some and you sleep some and you get up and start all over. Every now and then you get hit with hard times or good—who's to say? But then there are these tiny times in between when you look up at the tops of trees swaying or you sit down to a fine meal with a new family or you wake up alone and by the end of the day, you got yourself your first friend.

* * *

At my seat in the schoolhouse I look down at my slate board and I think and think. Each Monday we are to write a composition. So far our titles include "The Past," "Napoleon Bonaparte," and "A Snow Scene." Each Friday we have to memorize and recite a poem. "The Charge of the Light Brigade" by Alfred, Lord Tennyson. "A Psalm of Life" by Henry Wadsworth Longfellow. The title for our composition today is "Egypt."

I stare back down at my slate board. There is all that blank space that looks like my life. It is easier to look at that slate and think up funny things to do. It is easier to make mischief.

"Addy?" Mr. Frank says to me.

Everyone looks up.

"Just start. The words will come once you get started."

"I don't have any words for Egypt, Mr. Frank."

Mr. Frank, he thinks on this.

"Then write about your mother, Addy. Just talk to me. Write like you talk. Write everything you told me when we were working outside." He doesn't wait for me to complain. He just lets me sit there, picturing Momma kneeling in the front yard every morning to set up a new egg. I think of where she might be now. Somewhere in Texas where there's nothing but cowboys and tumbleweeds.

I don't follow Mr. Frank's advice. I don't want to bore him with what I already told him.

I set out to write. I write down the pictures in my head. I write about Momma and how she lifts her feet up feeling powerful whenever she wore her shoes. I write how Momma gave me sage and catnip to break my hives when I was a baby, and how later she showed me the ways to heal because, she told me, living amongst O'Donnells you need to know all the ways of healing.

I write about how right before he left, Pappy got into that brawl with Garner O'Donnell, the brother he plowed. I write how Garner shot Pappy. I write how exactly Momma sewed Pappy up and made a poultice of mullein and other healing herbs. And with that poultice, he left. Pappy up and left us.

I write and write. I write about Uncle Nub and Uncle Stick, who lived across the way from each other. Neither one of them had ears. I write until my hand hurts.

After the noon meal, while Mr. Frank naps against one of the bigger trees in the schoolyard, me and Little Bit drape a black snake across his ankles. All the schoolchildren stop the games they would not play with me. They come have themselves a look, and already they are giggling. The snake is dead, but Mr. Frank doesn't know that.

He wakes up all right and he keeps still the way you are supposed to around a snake. He lays there, waiting for it to slide away, and we children can hardly stand it. Maybe he hears someone giggle, or maybe he figures things out his own self, but when he sees that the snake is a might slow and it's not spitting out its forked tongue, licking its snake lips, Mr. Frank carefully lifts a stick and flips that snake fast. He sees that snake flop dead with a thud, and this is when we all laugh. Maybe Mr. Frank doesn't know what I know about snakes. King snakes and black snakes and green snakes aren't poisonous here. But watch out for a water moccasin, a copperhead, or a ground rattler. They are plenty harmful.

When we children see that Mr. Frank is not laughing, not even smiling, everyone around me runs and hides, leaving just me and Little Bit standing there.

Turns out Mr. Frank doesn't like the joke.

I can see from Mr. Frank's eyes that he wants to whup us both good, but he does not. He sits us down in seats in the front of the schoolhouse and he has me and Little Bit copy down over and over what he calls the golden rule: Do unto others as you would have them do unto you.

Then he takes Little Bit to the back of the room where I hear him whisper "Shameful."

I feel terrible bad about what I done. Mr. Frank and Miss Irene took me in on their wedding day, and what do I do? I lay a dead black snake across his legs. What kind of a thank-you is that?

How come being nasty comes so easy to me?

As I copy the words, I slip the heels of my feet out of my shoes. Mr. Frank gave me these shoes. He made them himself, and darn it all if they are not the hardest, stiffest, most uncomfortable things I ever wore. They are brown brogans that come up just above my ankle and they are no good for running or climbing. He made them from cowhide, tanned on his own place, but I slip them off and wiggle my toes in the air.

I think about No-Bob then, where I always went barefooted. My feet know the land there. I know the houses, the people—my people. I know every stream, field, tree, animal, and a good many rocks too. Not knowing such things here in this place, always having to consider right from wrong, wears me out. Every day there is so much thinking to do, figuring, conjecturing. And that is *outside* the schoolhouse.

On the walk home from school, Mr. Frank tells me he has read what I wrote today in school and he says I did a good job. At first I think he's talking about the golden rule lines, but then I remember the other things I wrote about No-Bob.

"I know it's hard for you to be away from your home and your people and everything that you know so well," he says. "It must be especially hard to learn new ways of doing things."

I stare at a magnolia tree then and notice the buds turning red, and it doesn't seem right or real that Momma's not seeing it too. These days feel mixed up because Momma's not here, not beside me looking, watching, telling me about the leaves on a magnolia and how they're so stiff and waxy, they almost never fall apart and come undone.

We pass the creek where we say bye to Little Bit, who walks alone the rest of her way home. Mr. Frank and I take a minute to wash our hands. I splash my face with water and rub hard on the scar that runs down the side of my nose. Dirt and water go there first and run through it like a river. I reach down to take a sip of water and catch a water beetle with my fingers, and something comes out of it because that water beetle stings me. I wonder if it hurt me because I hurt it.

"Come on, Addy," Mr. Frank says. "I'm hungry." He looks at me, takes a handkerchief from his pocket, dabs my face dry. I want to tell him how much I miss Momma, but I don't. We look at each other and smile. I guess me and Mr. Frank, we don't have to say much.

I set the water beetle in the water and turn it loose.

* * *

That night Miss Irene confides that she has not gotten much sleep of late because she is not used to sharing her bed with Mr. Frank, who kicks in his sleep. I decide to help out.

In the middle of the night, I sneak into their room and tie Mr. Frank's big toe to the bedpost just like Momma done me once to keep me from kicking her. But the next morning when Mr. Frank gets up and trips and falls because he didn't know his toe was hooked up with the bed, neither he nor Miss Irene think I've helped.

At school, we relearn some about the war. It all started because Pierre Gustave Toutant Beauregard fired the first shot, a man with a too-long name. We look at pictures of Ulysses S. Grant. I always did think Mr. Grant was a might better-looking than Robert E. Lee, but I keep that bit to myself.

Then, finally, we put the past behind us and we begin a new subject called geography. Mr. Frank stands in front of the schoolroom with his nose bandaged up from his fall just that morning. He shows us a map from a book called *Atlas,* and it is there that we children see the world all charted out. On the page, in this book, the lines are so clear. There is the United States of America with the shapes of each state marked with straight lines, but when you get up close, they squiggle here and there. There are lines for rivers and jig jags for mountains.

"There's still a lot of room here," I say, pointing to the West, wide open and unlined.

"Yes, there is, Addy." With the bandage and his nose all plugged up, he talks like he has a cold. "Many go out there to seek their fortunes and maybe even mark the land with their own names."

"Didn't your grandpa go out west?" Rew Smith asks Mr. Frank.

"Yes, he did, Rew. To Texas."

"That's where my pappy went." For a minute, me and Mr. Frank, we look at each other. This might be the first thing we have in common. I wonder if he misses his grandpa like I do my momma and pappy.

"Where's No-Bob? Where's Smith County? Where are all our roads and rivers?" Little Bit wants to know.

"They're not on this map. A lot of the smaller places don't get put on a big map like this. But there are the big rivers here." Mr. Frank, he points out all the big rivers. He calls them sources for the little rivers. He says if a river forgets its source, it dries up. He points to the river Strong. I remember what Little Bit told me. Their slave, Buck, crossed that river called Strong.

Mr. Frank, he starts explaining our assignment. He says he'd like each of us to decide on a place and make a map of it. It can be our house, our neighborhood, our town, or even a road.

"Draw it out like you see here," Mr. Frank says. "Write the names of the rivers and paths if you know them. Write down what you know about this place. You can work individually or with partners." I have a feeling that today Mr. Frank wants us to do our work and leave him alone. Especially me.

"How long do we have?" Little Bit wants to know. Already we know we'll be partners. We're leaning forward ready to run out of the schoolhouse. I want to take Little Bit where I know no one else goes. We want to map uncharted territory.

Mr. Frank eyes us all there in the room. His eyes look puffy from the fall. He should be more careful when he gets out of bed.

"You got two days."

We children scatter, making big plans to chart out our own slice of Smith County.

* * *

Late that afternoon, Little Bit and me walk home with Mr. Frank. At the creek, Little Bit goes her own way toward her own house. As we near our house, Mr. Frank perks up when he sees who's on the front porch.

"Well, look who we have here. Addy, come meet an old friend of mine, Tempy." A small-headed, red-haired man and a pretty sand-colored woman sit on the front porch with Miss Irene, sipping coffee.

Mr. Frank makes the introductions. The pretty sand-colored woman is called Zula and she looks to be full-blooded Choctaw. She looks at me and says, "I know you," and I look back and say, "I don't think so."

She is expecting a baby and I'm guessing she's this Mr. Tempy's wife. I have never seen nor thought of a white man marrying a Choctaw woman. I think of what Pappy and Momma would say, how they would call her a bone picker, how they would wonder about this Mr. Tempy, but still, I can't help but wonder why such a pretty lady would marry that small-headed, red-haired man.

No one says so, but it appears this Mr. Tempy has traveled a ways. Miss Irene says he lives in a place on the Leaf River right outside Taylorsville.

They are on their way to Mobile to drive the fattest hogs I

ever seen and sell one hundred dollars' worth. He has brought sweet potatoes and cornmeal from a barrel marked u.s. He says years ago the federal government put him in charge of distributing federal food because they didn't trust the Confederates, but the food was so slow to get down south, most everyone has forgotten about it by now.

"If you're not a Confederate," I say, "does that make you a Yankee?"

Mr. Frank laughs and says the war's over, but he looks at Mr. Tempy to see what he says.

"I'm neither Confederate nor Yankee, Miss Addy, though I once fought for the feds. Not everyone can be so easily divided into two groups of either-or. Some would call me a deserter, but I believe I've deserted no one. I'm for peace. I'm for family. Period."

"I think my momma told me about the likes of you," I say. "You one of those Jones County deserters?"

"Who might your momma be?"

"She's an O'Donnell," Mr. Frank says, as though this should explain everything, and that gets me riled.

"She says about three hundred well-armed deserters have a little town called the Free State of Jones," I say. "She says you all are traitors and you all should be shot."

"Addy," Mr. Frank says.

"Addy, you're being rude to our guests," Miss Irene says. "You come inside with me this instant."

"No, no. She's fine," Mr. Tempy says. "Miss Addy, I would love for you to pay us a visit where we live under the tall pines and canebrakes. Be our guest. Besides, most of the folks you call deserters have moved on. Mostly it's a few of us and the Choctaw. We're free of everything there. Free of judgments from family, friends, and foes. Come whenever you'd like. I think you might like it there."

"Yes, sir," I say. "Thank you kindly. But I have supper to tend to." I go inside and start fixing up the cornbread. I'm flustered, the way I see some chickens are sometimes, and I'm not sure why.

From inside, I can hear Mr. Frank telling Mr. Tempy about the general store he wants to start. Mr. Frank would have to take regular runs to New Orleans for supplies. Mr. Tempy says he'd be happy to go along with him—safety in numbers, he says. He goes off for a while about the great cities of America before and after the war—Charleston, Natchez, Chicago, and more. Mr. Tempy says traveling now can be dangerous. You have to carry a gun, always loaded. Bandits and thieves are on the road, at the ready, knowing you're loaded with either cash or supplies. They don't just take. They kill too. I walk over toward the open door to hear Mr. Tempy whisper about a story I already know. Two brothers rob men, rip open their bellies, take out their entrails, then stuff the bodies with stones or sand to sink them in the rivers.

"That'd be the Harpe brothers," I say, walking out onto the porch. I want them to get this right. "That all happened on the Natchez Trace way before the war and they're both long dead. I know some say the O'Donnells did that, but those were the Harpes, and they cut off Big Harpe's head and nailed it in the fork of a tree out near Robertson's Lick."

Mr. Frank and Mr. Tempy stare at me. "It's true," I say. "Then some old woman went and took that old Harpe head years later because she needed to pulverize the bones of a human skull for some remedy."

Mr. Tempy laughs.

"It's not make-believe," I say. "It's all true, what they say. My pappy says those Harpe brothers were as mean as the stories say."

Miss Irene skirts me away and says we got some cooking to do.

"You think she knows whatever happened to that Little Harpe, Wiley?" Mr. Tempy asks Mr. Frank.

I shout behind me, "He joined up with Mason's gang and got put on trial in New Orleans." Miss Irene slams the door shut, but I yell through it. "They cut off his little head too. Stuck it on a pole along the trace, north of Rodney." Then I open the door a crack and listen.

"For Pete's sake, Tempy. Don't encourage her," I hear Mr. Frank say. "You think she knows as many good stories as she knows bad?"

"Aw, come on now, Frank," Mr. Tempy says. "She's still got both ears, both eyes. She hasn't done anything wrong yet."

"Yet," Mr. Frank says. "I can't get her to print her name properly, but she knows words like *entrails.*"

"Yeah, well, at least she's heard about a court system. She might be the only O'Donnell who has. You *could* send her away. Heard tell about a nunnery in Baton Rouge," Mr. Tempy says, but I don't listen to the rest.

I will run away before I ever get sent to a nunnery in Baton Rouge.

Miss Irene and Zula are fixing up a supper. Zula is very quiet as she works. She doesn't say a word as she pulls apart a chicken so that Miss Irene can cook it.

Miss Irene doesn't have me do all we did for Mr. Frank's ma and pa way back in May, but we do put out a fine spread of food all the same. Zula doesn't eat with the men. Miss Irene tells me that it's her custom to eat separate, so she and I eat with Zula a ways away from Mr. Frank and Mr. Tempy. Zula is small but strong-looking with her dark hair, dark eyebrows, and wide nose. Her brown eyes are set apart and she looks smart to me. She and I sneak peeks at each other. She eats small bits at a time. I eat big chunks.

Mr. Frank and Mr. Tempy eat every last crumb. After our meal, Miss Irene says she wants to make a custard for later on. She takes Zula with her to gather eggs from the hen house.

"Howdy do, Shanks." I recognize the voice. Outside, Mr. Smith sets up high on his horse and doesn't come down. His redheaded boy, Rew, the boy I sit beside at school, sits on the horse behind his father. Mr. Smith only has the one leg. He lost the other at the Battle of Tupelo. His wife, Tid Smith, stands aside her husband's horse. She looks tired and worn out, but when she sees us on the porch, she eyes Mr. Tempy in the queerest way.

Mr. Smith, he tips his hat and says, "Hey, Miss Addy." I say hey and look at Mr. Frank and Mr. Tempy, feeling good again about myself. Mr. Smith and my pappy fought together. Mr. Smith told me once that Pappy was a great soldier because he wouldn't submit to the rules in army life. He says Pappy was brave on duty but sometimes left camp without permission, so he was called before a court-martial and sentenced to death. Pappy stood at his gravesite, awaiting the firing squad, when Mr. Smith says he interceded on his behalf and saved his life.

I don't understand why his son, Rew, lies and says that his father says such terrible things about the O'Donnells.

"I see you got company." Mr. Smith leans close to see who else is on the porch. Mr. Tempy steps forward then.

"Don't I know you?" Mr. Smith says to Mr. Tempy.

"I don't believe so," Mr. Tempy says, smiling.

I seen the looks on lots of men's faces in No-Bob just before a brawl, usually right after Sunday church, when the men go down to the creek to water their horses and pass the bottle. Put a few O'Donnell men together with a bottle, and before too long, you got a fight. I seen the way an O'Donnell man looks before he's fixing to cut someone, and that is the look on Mr. Smith's face right now.

"You want to come in, sit a spell?" Mr. Frank says. I 'spect Mr. Frank seen the look on Mr. Smith's face too.

"No, sir. I just come to pay you a visit, Frank. Already stopped and spoke with your pa. I have some business to discuss."

I wonder why Miss Irene and Zula aren't coming out to the porch to greet Mr. Smith. They stay inside the hen house, peeking out every now and then.

"Addy," Mr. Tempy says. "Show me where the well is. I'm powerful thirsty."

"What kind of business?" Mr. Frank says to Mr. Smith. Mrs. Smith and Rew just stand aside like they're not even there.

I know Mr. Tempy knows where the well is because he fetched the first bucket of water for Miss Irene, but I lead him over there all the same.

I walk real slow so I can hear what Mr. Smith's got to say. I hear, "Shanks, you're one of our best wide-awake citizens." I hear, "You and I both know niggers ain't supposed to always know right from wrong. They ain't got masters anymore to teach 'em." I hear Mr. Frank say that the Bible doesn't say anything about slavery being right. "You know that," he says. I hear Mr. Smith say, "Right or wrong, with deadly fear, we dread the possibility of Negro rule." I hear, "We're here to help. You should join up and help too, Frank. You missed the war, Frank. Don't miss this. You're a good Christian, ain't you?"

I am still wearing the shoes that I am not used to. They pinch my heels and I would rather be barefooted. These here shoes are the hardest shoes. I can't bend them so much as crack them. I will wear out before they ever get soft.

"I was no secessionist, I will tell the truth about it, Addy," Mr. Tempy says. "Some of these boys thought it was big to get the big guns on. Not me." He pulls up the bucket of well water and drinks, then wipes his mouth with his sleeve.

"My momma was only telling me what my pappy says." I tell Mr. Tempy that when I first heard about Mr. Lincoln, I thought he was partly God, but Pappy set me straight. He says Mr. Lincoln was more devil than God.

"What else did yer pappy say about us?" His hogs are in the pen nearby, sniffing around.

"Y'all are nothing more than a band of criminals. You got a hideout?"

He looks me up and down. "Maybe."

"You got treasure? Like pirates?" I head on over to the smokehouse. I need to get the dirt into barrels, and while I do this, Mr. Tempy helps, and he tells me a story about a man named Newt Knight who was a poor man, and even though he didn't own any Negroes, he thought that the twenty-Negro law wasn't fair, that it enabled the rich men who had at least twenty slaves to avoid serving in the army and that the Confederacy wasn't right to ask him to risk his life for people who rated themselves so far above him. So this man, Newt Knight, stayed behind and camped out on the Leaf River. Some call it Deserters' Den. He stayed there all during the Civil War. Some say there is Yankee treasure soldiers brought back from all over buried all around Knight's camp.

I pour water over the dirt. After we boil it down, we will have salt. Cornmeal without salt is hardly worth eating. Salt is up to ten cents a pound and Mr. Frank isn't going to New Orleans or the coast anytime soon.

"All I know is if there was a war right now, I'd join up." I put away our shovels and slap my hands to get rid of the salty smokehouse dirt.

"Now, Addy, why in the deuce would you say that?"

"I'm from No-Bob, Mr. Tempy, and if I went off to war, I'd get far, far away from danger."

Mr. Tempy laughs but I don't because what I'm saying is the truth and he and I both know it.

"That's *funny,* Addy," he says. "Don't you *ever* laugh?"

"I laughed in my brain," I say.

Some of Mr. Tempy's hogs begin to squeal. I look at Mr. Tempy and plug my nose. "They stink."

We see Mr. Smith stepping down from the porch, his pole leg thunking on the planks. He yells back to Mr. Frank, "You hear say, 'Don't wait for six strong men to take you to church'? Well, then, don't wait for six strong men to take you to join up, you hear?" He hauls himself, then his wife and son, up on his horse, leans in, and giddyups.

Mr. Tempy and me, we go back up to the house.

"You best be careful, Frank," Mr. Tempy says. "I sure hope me and the missus being here didn't cause you any trouble."

"No trouble."

"You know about this club he's talking about don't you?"

"He's calling it a Christian group. All men."

"A Christian group." Mr. Tempy spits a wad of chewing tobacco. "Oh, yeah. All good people. White men who go to church and work hard. Good family men. Oh, they're not against anyone. Except Indians, Jews, coloreds, and anybody not like themselves." The way Mr. Tempy is talking makes me think he is joshing. Makes me think he's not calling it straight. This Mr. Tempy is like no other person I met. He says something funny, but his face is so serious. He has my head all full of confusions.

"Trouble, are they?" Mr. Frank says to Mr. Tempy.

"They're called the Ku Klux Klan, Frank," Mr. Tempy says, all business now. "White men who ride around on horseback at night scaring all the freed slaves. They're up to no good."

Zula comes out of the hen house and stands beside Mr. Tempy, who puts his arm around her.

"That Anglo man, he is full of loud noise and words." It's the second time I've heard her talk.

"Frank," Miss Irene calls out from the hen house. "Someone's taken all the eggs and someone's done stole one of our chickens."

Mr. Frank and Mr. Tempy, the two of them both, they look at me.

The chicken thief could have been a fox or a mink or a skunk. But I don't wait to hear. I have no interest in such things as talk of chicken thieves and trouble. I head up the road to Mr. Frank's ma and pa's house to find Little Bit, so we can go chart out our own little bit of Smith County.

Little Bit wants me to take her to No-Bob so we can map it, but I say no, no, not on your life. I have other plans than to cross back into No-Bob. I reckon we need to map out better, more uncharted territory. I tell Little Bit there's treasure to be found.

Before we set out, we stop by Mr. Frank's house where Mr.

Tempy is still talking a mean streak. I hide red pepper in Mr. Tempy's chewing tobacco. We stay long enough to catch the look on his face after the first two chews. His watery, bulging eyes catch mine and I say bye.

Then Little Bit and me, we gather up paper and some charcoal pencils, and we set out for our great adventure to find Mr. Tempy's buried treasure.

Chapter 5

We follow the road through the woods that smell of pine and toadstools, lichen and moss. These woods are dense, but if you know them, you know their paths—same ones the animals use. And I wouldn't mind now if Nona Dewitt or Rew Smith called me an animal. Animals are smart.

Cobwebs catch in our hair and we laugh, pulling at the sticky strings.

"Let's be spies like they done in the war," Little Bit says.

"OK, but who are we spying on and who are we spying for?"

"It doesn't matter," she says, all smiles. "Let's just *spy!*"

"Hey, let's you and me make a map leading to Tempy's hideout."

"Yeah!" Little Bit squeals. "Maybe there's hidden treasure like you said."

"Yeah," I say. I'm just as riled as she is.

I got me some big happies. We are outside and away from all that ugly talk of thieves and thieving. So much talk going on. But now we are outside. Outside! We are searching for treasure. We will draw us a map and put down all that we know. The setting sun is blinking off the tops of the shiny magnolia leaves and the air is cool and crisp.

After a while, me and Little Bit, we turn off and walk the Choctaw trail that I know to be the Three-Chopped Wat Trail. We breathe in the smell of rotten leaves and squashed persimmons. We find juniper berries and paint our faces with the juices. We play hide-the-switch and Bugger Bear, but as the light fades our make-believe games get too scary for the both of us.

This road here is a trail not many know about. My pappy shown me. He would take this instead of the one main road out of town to catch the train out of Mize to New Orleans—that is the one most traveled. I think of Mr. Frank's talk of going to New Orleans for provisions for his general store.

Bandits and thieves still prowl up and down the main road. Everyone, like Mr. Tempy, is still telling tales about the Natchez Trace and all the famous ruffians who preyed on travelers, thieving and killing, laughing all the while.

I look around now. This little trail is cleared almost to the width of a carriage road by horses' hoofs and people's feet. More people than I thought must know of it. On either side of us, thick, uncut longleaf pines come right up to the road, and with all that thick, tangled underbrush and dense canebrakes, there's no telling what all or who all is in there, hiding. I hear tell of wildcats in canebrakes.

If I was the type of person to get spooked, I would be spooked, but I am not that type of a person.

"How you be, Little Bit?"

"I'm just fine, Addy." Her teeth glow whiter against her red, berry-stained skin.

The wind blows through the dried cane and makes a mournful sound. I am glad there is still light out, but it is fading.

"If you get scared, just sing, OK?"

"Don't worry about me. I like to be scared. Ever wonder why us children like to get scared?"

"What should we sing?" I say. "How 'bout we could make something up?"

“All right then,” Little Bit says. She sings a funny tune about a kitten, and if there’s a key, neither one of us can find it. Little Bit can’t carry a tune in a bucket.

While she sings, she takes the folded paper from her dress pocket. She unfolds the paper and starts to draw the map while I keep an eye out for chestnuts and treasure. Momma says food and money are the only two things on an O’Donnell mind. Good thing my mission keeps me from getting spooked.

Already, Little Bit has drawn our winding road with a line that looks to be a snake. She is marking it with the trees we see, even putting in some squirrels and birds.

We stop at the cemetery for the black folk so Little Bit can stand there and draw that in too. Most all the markers or stones are gone and there are just places where there are graves that are sunken in.

“Did you know Miss Tiller?” Little Bit says.

“No,” I say. “I don’t know many of the black folk in Smith.”

Little Bit walks up and down the graveyard telling the stories of everybody she knows. I think, *How does she know all these people?* I think, *I only know white O’Donnells.* I don’t know any of the people in this here graveyard.

I think of Mr. Frank’s map up at the schoolhouse. What Momma and Pappy had between them—that fierce love—was not on that map. All the jokes I played on Mr. Frank were not on that map. The war was not on that map, and neither was the surrender. What is on a map, what does get recorded, and the way things look don't have much to do with what's going on with people. That makes me happy and sad—happy because I know the streams will keep streaming and the skies will keep clouding and clearing, even as we people fight and tear and claw at each other. But the big world going about its business no matter what we do makes me sad too because what difference do we make? Looking around me, at all the graves and leftover destruction—seems we just keep on messing up a darned good thing.

Little Bit gives me the pencil and I write down the names she calls out. I write what all I know too. Every place has a name. Every name has a story. My letters turn out better.

We both hear singing that's a might bit better than mine or Little Bit's.

"Hey, look," Little Bit says. "The black folks got church going at the schoolhouse. Let's go listen."

I heard about this schoolhouse, but I have never seen it. This schoolhouse was built after the war for any free slave who wanted an education. They used the schoolhouse for their church services same as us.

You never can tell about church because you never can tell about the preacher. Seems to me a church is only as good as its preacher. One year in No-Bob, a passing preacher called for a foot-washing. I got stuck with Stump O'Donnell's feet, and by the time church was over, his feet were still black. It was so nasty that afterward, we all of us complained, and even the preacher had to admit that the duty of washing the feet should be performed in a private capacity only.

Little Bit and me listen to the black folks singing "Steal Away."

Up at our school, Mr. Frank said that before the war was over, on the day of emancipation, most all the field hands were called in and told they were free. White folks told their field hands they had to boss their own business, told them it was up to them to find their own work. If they wanted to stay on, they'd get paid, but most never did get paid. Most went into debt. They got turned loose without nothing.

I never knew much about freedom or slavery myself. None of the O'Donnells could afford slaves, but they would have had them if they could have.

I think I understand why some of the colored folk stayed and keep on staying. They're like me. They don't know anywhere else like they know home. And so many of the ones who stayed were old, past the time when a body can move on. They stay and they do the same thing they did before the war, when they were slaves, but now they work for money or land that they never seem to get. They stay with their freedom. Their free is inside their heads and I can't help but wonder if that is free enough.

Inside the schoolhouse they must be having a baptizing, because the preacher is talking about baptizing and saying how Baptist is the only real religion. He's saying a while back everybody had to offer up sacrifices, a goat or a sheep or something. But Jesus come and changed all that. He says, "Father, I'll die for them." But why did he go and die for people who were poking and prodding him, sticking thorns on top his head, filling his dry mouth with vinegar? Who would die for such a sorry lot? And so it was that he became a sacrifice.

My brain itches, thinking on what the preacher is saying. Our sacrifice, his father's sacrifice, or Jesus's, I cannot figure which.

"Presbyterians don't go down under the water like Baptists do," Little Bit whispers.

Soon enough they start singing my favorite, that song called "Old-Time Religion."

This singing is so good that Little Bit and I stay on until

the end. When they all come out, Little Bit waves after one of the little boys I recognize. Jess Still. He comes running over and we all three say hey.

He laughs when he sees Little Bit.

"You're red, Little Bit!"

She laughs, painting his cheek with a leftover juniper berry. "You're purple."

He's small and I see the asafetida he wears round his neck in a little bag.

"Can I smell?" I say, pointing to the bag.

He nods, telling me his ma, Early Rise, gave him the bag to keep him from having asthma, smallpox, measles, and any other diseases.

"I used to have one too." The herbs together smell sagey and sweet.

"Guess your momma figure you don't need one anymore now that you're grown up and safe from disease."

"Maybe," I say. "Maybe not."

He looks me over. He has what my momma used to call a traveling eye. His one eye stays fixed while his other eye roams. I think on how handy that would be, how it would keep you safe.

Jess lifts the bag off his neck, then puts it around my neck. "There," he says. "Now you're safe."

"What about you?" Little Bit says.

"Momma will make me another one."

He asks me my name and I tell him.

"Addy," he repeats after me. "Sounds like Adam. What's it short for?"

"You're the first person in the whole world who ever asked me that," I say, smiling. "It's short for Adeline, but nobody ever calls me that."

"Then *I* will," Jess says. "Wanna race, Miss Adeline?"

And we do. Back and forth, the three of us run and run just for fun.

Mr. Tempy and Zula leave the following day, way before sunup. They want to get an early start so they can get a good amount of cash for their hogs in Mobile. That night, me and Little Bit, we go back to that little schoolhouse church, and we keep going back almost every night after that like it's our very own treasure. The first few times we use our map to make our way back, but after a while, we know the way by heart. Seems like every night they're singing, or listening to the preacher, or having some kind of get-together. And every time we go, Jess Still is there, happy to see us.

I tell him he's lucky because they have such a good preacher.

"But every time he starts, I fall to sleep. Every time," he says, snapping his fingers. "Like clockwork, Miss Adeline."

Jess Still reminds me of me before I met Mr. Frank and Miss Irene, only Jess is happier because his ma and pa aren't like mine. He doesn't wear shoes and he talks the way he talks without anybody bothering to correct him. We catch crickets and butterflies and then turn them loose. We three soak our feet in the creek. He teaches us the words to the church songs we like best. Because Jess's ma made him and Little Bit both a new asafetida bag, we three even smell alike. In no time flat, Jess Still is my second friend.

On Sunday there is the biggest crowd, and Little Bit and I stay just to hear the extra-special good singing.

But then all at once, in the middle of an amen, we hear horses and men shouting. I hear a familiar man-voice, but I can't place it. I hear him say, "We have to fight for our life, boys, more desperately than at Shiloh and Vicksburg. What is called for here is loyalty, courage, and grim determination."

"Well, peas and rice," Little Bit says. "It's just getting good. What is it now?"

Little Bit is right. The singing is just getting good, when out of the woods come these folks wearing old Confederate uniforms and white or dark gray cloth masks over their heads with cut-out spook faces. At first we want to laugh at the cut-out eye, nose, and mouth holes, but then we see that these men are not here for fun but to do something mighty fearsome, and too soon they begin to foul the air with curses.

"It's them Ku Kluxers that Mr. Tempy was talking to Mr. Frank about a while back," I whisper.

At the hem of a long patch of tall grass, we duck under the scrub bushes and get a good look at the passing men. And I am relieved to see that they are just men. These are not the spooks they mean to appear to be. Nor are they wildcats or worse. They are just men. White men, all of them.

Some of the men get down off their horses. Some of the men stay on their horses, howling and yelping and shouting out ugly things. The men on the ground set to work. They take a pine log over thirty feet high and lash another, shorter arm to it. They set the big pole into the ground and there stands before us the tallest cross I ever seen. They soak burlap bags in turpentine I can smell, then they wrap the bags all around the wood.

It is dark and hard to see. I move closer.

"Addy, don't," Little Bit whispers. "We don't know those men. We don't know what they would do to us."

"What about Jess?" I say. "Where is he?"

"He's inside," Little Bit whispers.

The wind starts up, the clouds clear, and the moonlight lights up what there is to see. One man has the fanciest hood, with extra slits above the eyes, mouth, and nose, like worry lines. He crouches, then lights a match, and the flame lights up the mask of his hood and all the worry lines look like so many lit-up rivers.

Something is happening here. Something else, above all that happened before. I can smell it the way I can smell a rain coming. The air has changed.

"We should tell Jess to stay inside," I say.

"Addy, no," Little Bit says, pulling me back into the thicket. "His ma and pa are with him."

Some of the men on horses hear us and turn our way to look.

I see the man with the match stand and look around toward us. He is a tall, powerful-built man and I want to run to him, push him down, and say why? Why would you burn a cross? Why would you turn something good into something bad?

It feels as though the ground is dropping out from under my feet, and the feeling is not funny the way it should be. Did everything change as fast as all that, in the time it took for this man to light that match?

How can good be made evil in so short a time?

The tall man drops the lit match on the burlap bags. The wind picks up and the fire takes off fast up and down the pole that quickly turns black and brittle. The men on horseback and on foot now stand back to look at the fire as the wind blows harder. Little Bit and me both stand because no one is looking our way. Everyone is facing the fire. Someone yells, "Timber!" in a joking way, and sure enough, the whole cross comes tumbling down and down and down onto the roof of the schoolhouse. Part of the roof caves in. Part of the roof catches on fire.

People come screaming out, but we can't see Jess.

"Jess!" I scream.

Little Bit yells, "Is that him?"

It is so hard to see.

We are looking as more and more people come running out of the schoolhouse.

It seems like the whole world is on fire just then. I look up and down the road. Where is help? Isn't anyone going to come and help?

One hooded man goes into the burning schoolhouse as though to help and drags out a colored man who is coughing something terrible. This man with the hood does what so many masters in these parts done to their slaves before the war. He tears off this man's half-burned shirt, and while someone holds him down, he whips this man. He uses a strap with holes in it, so that they raise big blisters. He is mean the way I seen O'Donnells be mean. Mean the way I seen Uncle "Tiptoe" be mean, when he whipped a man who had strayed into No-Bob till the blood came, then had somebody else anoint the man's flesh with red pepper and turpentine.

What's to be done with all that you know and see? What do you do with so much meanness in this sorrowful world?

Some of the men under their masks are laughing. *Laughing.* They are *happy.* They are having *fun.* They use their good singing voices to sing a nasty song about how they would be back to see all the black people, how they were coming back to get them all. Everyone around them is screaming and running and shouting and crying, and these hooded men are whooping and having themselves a big time.

More and more people from the schoolhouse come pouring out, coughing, yelling, screaming, crying. There are babies here. Children. Where is Jess?

What is happening to us?

Little Bit is crying, not looking at what I'm looking at. She is looking at me. She is saying, *Addy O'Donnell, if you go out there now, you will get us both killed.*

What does this look like on a map? I think of what the fire might look like from way high above. It would be small but hard to miss. I used to think about Jesus ascending into heaven and I wondered exactly how long that took. And how long does it take to descend? To come back down and help out, maybe even fix a few things that have gone and broke or just plain come undone.

We are falling backwards, back before our mommas, teachers, and preachers taught us how to be good, back into a dark, muddy time before we knew better. What is happening?

The wind picks up again and blows the fire to make more fire. It's dry. We haven't had rain in over a month. The leaves blow around, and with the wind going the way it's going, it doesn't take long for the fire to spread from the roof to the entire schoolhouse, and all at once the whole building is ablaze and lit up, hot and powerful and awful. Even the hooded men stop what they are doing to stand in awe of the flames.

Some of them hitch up their horses, ready to leave.

"My baby. My baby. Where's my baby? Jess? Jess Still, where are you, boy?" Jess's momma, Early Rise, runs back and forth across the schoolyard and I can't help it no longer. I run out of the bushes and Little Bit comes running out after me, saying, "No, Addy. Don't."

I run into the flames and smoke and right there, in the back of the schoolhouse, there lies Jess Still, looking like he's fast asleep.

He looks smaller than small and his right hand is closed around the asafetida he wears round his neck. He doesn't feel heavy when I pick him up and put him over my shoulder. The smoke and fire make me mad and my mad makes me strong.

I get out of there fast, and when I fall down to the ground with Jess Still I am coughing and spitting. Early Rise comes and hugs her boy but he does not wake. Someone pours water on him but he does not wake. Early Rise is wailing. She cannot get her little boy Jess Still to wake up.

I am too late. I was too late. He is gone. Jess is gone. Not from the fire, but from breathing in all that smoke. I kneel down there with all of them wailing. I hold on to the asafetida bag, the one he gave me.

Little Bit pulls me away. Little Bit, streaked now with dirt and tears. We run run run back home to Mr. Frank's. When we get there they are both either too angry or too shocked to start yelling at us for coming home so late. Little Bit tells her brother to go go go to the colored church and help them. We can't explain. There are no words. They smell the smoke on us. We say yes, fire, fire.

Mr. Frank goes and Miss Irene stays and lights a fire for heat.

Little Bit and me, we get out and unfold our map. It is on a big sheet of paper, the kind Miss Irene uses to wrap things in. Little Bit and me, we both know what to do. We set out to draw. We do it together, side by side, not her at one end and me at the other, because we want to make sure we get all the little things right. We mark the trails we used more carefully. We draw trees we remember more clearly. We label them too, because when you chart it all out at the end of the day, it's important to see everything from far off and up close too. Most people miss the up-close, little things.

We sit together side by side and draw what we've just seen.

It seems so important. We are both in a hurry because we both know. We both have to remember this so that we can forget.

We draw and draw. We draw the map and with it we draw the story. And not once do we stop. We draw the schoolhouse and the fire. We draw all the hooded men. We draw the cross.

We draw the man with the special hood lighting the match. Little Bit marks it with the date.

We fold up the map. We put it in a jar that had the good peaches. Then we go outside, dig a hole under Mr. Frank's praying log, put it there in the ground, cover it back up with dirt, then roll the log over it.

Buried. Not our treasure, our nightmare.

Chapter 6

I keep thinking about the colored graveyard down the road. There were no markings for the graves, or if there ever had been, they are long gone. I never made a headstone before. I sit outside on a log with Little Bit and her brother Jack. We are here with all the rest who come to mourn Jess Still. I think about what a headstone should say about this little boy.

Jess Still Rise, named on account of his standing still all the time, even though we three did all that running in the woods. When I met him that first time, when he and his pappy drove the wagon to Mr. Frank's house, I wished I'd been him. He had a pappy to ride with.

He was the only person who ever called me Adeline.

"What else did you know about Jess?" I whisper to Little Bit. We are all supposed to be quiet now, thinking and praying. Jess Still lays in a pine box in front of us. They made his coffin at home and blackened it with soot. We have services outside because the schoolhouse was this town's one building and it is now burned to the ground.

Little Bit thinks some. "When he was littler, he used to leave out the *g*'s on all his *-ing* words."

I am both glad and sad to know this about my friend.

The black folks sing and it is slow and sad, the pitifullest and mournfullest song I ever heard. Mr. Frank and his parents, Miss Irene, Little Bit, Jack, and me are the only white folks here. Mr. Frank's ma and pa brought Early Rise a ham. They said they didn't know what else to do—they felt so terrible bad for Early Rise and her husband, Sunny. They said they know what it is to lose a son.

The preacher is the preacher from that night, a black man who speaks in a calm, quiet way. No shouting, ranting or raving, or speaking in tongues the way I seen some preachers do. He just speaks to us, like he is talking to me personal and from his heart. Like he's talking to his brother or his sister, his son or his daughter, like he cares.

I look at each of the people as they come up to say goodbye to Jess Still. There is a former slave woman named Please Cook with her son, Deuteronomy. She puts a kerchief inside Jess's open coffin. A man named John Calhoun steps up, kneels down on one knee, and stays with Jess for some time.

Little Bit whispers to me about Mr. Calhoun. Before the war was over, his mistress agreed to grant Mr. Calhoun freedom for one thousand dollars. Mr. Calhoun worked after he'd finish his day's work. He was good with his hands and made walking sticks and split rails by moonlight. On days off he made cabinets and sold them to the white people. He saved nine hundred dollars and gave it to his owner, but before he could make an additional one hundred dollars, the slaves were freed. Without asking, Mr. Calhoun's mistress gave him a deed to forty acres of land, because, she said, that's what he had paid for. I suppose she thought she was doing right by Mr. Calhoun, but what if he didn't want the land at all? What if he just wanted to leave?

Mr. Calhoun stands and places a little hand-carved wooden ark in Jess's right hand.

I recognize some from the schoolhouse, others I don't.

There is the black man without a hand. Heard tell he was trying to read and write and his master cut his hand off. He's carrying a Bible with his one hand and he reaches in and leaves that book with Jess. They all have something to give Jess, for where he's going in that sweet afterlife, there's no telling what he'll need.

Then the people sing "Been Toilin' at the Hill So Long" while Jess's momma lays a new asafetida bag in Jess's left hand.

I'm so sad I can't cry.

It is like I see them all for the first time and my heart is heavy, heavy with hurt and worry for what I seen, what I see now, and what I know. This feeling I have is bigger than the sad feeling I have had for Momma and Pappy. I grieve so much that my heart feels heavy in my breast.

"Are you for religion?"

"Well, sure I am, Addy," Little Bit whispers.

"Is there a heaven for colored people?"

"I suppose there is."

"What's it look like?"

"Can't rightly tell. Never been to any of the heavens. And I'm in no hurry neither."

"Y'all need to hush," little Jack says.

The O'Donnells, we don't bury our dead on public

ground. We bury our dead on our own farms. The land is tilled over our graves.

Little Bit and I get to talking about ghosts. I say Jesus came back and spoke to his friends, the Apostles, after he died. Didn't that make him a ghost? Little Bit says it makes him a holy ghost.

"Do you hear them talking during prayers?" little Jack says to his ma, trying to get me and Little Bit in trouble.

The night of the fire, after I put Jess Still before her, Early Rise took her son and had him stretched out just like you see Mary done with Jesus Christ when they took him down off the cross. And they all sat down by his body on the ground and cried cried cried like Mary and them done. That's the way Little Bit and me left them that night. That's the way I'll always remember them.

The grave of Jess Still is not mine to mark. That is for his family. Even this makes me sad. Why must we all claim somebody, dead or alive? When a body dies, is it free or does it belong to God? When is a body free? How do we *be* free? Do we all need to be taught to be free?

Almost every family loses a baby here in these parts. But not like this. Babies aren't murdered. Nobody knows what to say. Are there any words for comfort?

After we put Jess Still in that sorry red ground, Mr. Frank, Miss Irene, and I head home in the wagon. Little Bit and Jack go home with Mr. Frank's pa and ma.

I think maybe they don't want me around Little Bit anymore. I think maybe they think she's seen too much on account of me. And I feel sorrowful bad about that, but I also want to say she's her own person. She is just now teaching herself to be free.

After we eat, none of us saying much, I go out near the barn to sit on Mr. Frank's praying log, but Mr. Frank is already there. He's reading his Bible, trying to find some story to keep his mood company.

Mr. Frank, he scoots over and doesn't say anything when I sit down. The log sinks a little with my weight.

"I'm sorry that you and Little Bit saw that little boy Jess die in that fire," he says. "I spoke with the sheriff. They're going to look for the men who did this."

When Mr. Frank came back from the fire that night, Little Bit and me, we told him all that we knew. Later, after Little Bit fell to sleep, I went outside, dug up the peach jar, unfolded the map, and stared and stared and stared at that man lighting the match that lit the cross that fell on the schoolhouse that killed Jess Still. Then I folded the map back up and put it in the jar and into the hole under the log.

"Do you think they'll ever find the men that did it?"

"Hard to say," Mr. Frank says, sighing. He looks tired and pale. "Sheriff says there have been a lot of bad nights. A lot of violence mostly aimed at the freed slaves."

"You're not joining up with them Ku Kluxers, are you, Mr. Frank?"

"Course not, Addy. And you don't need to worry about these things."

"If I don't, who will?"

"You did a fine thing, going in after Jess. A fine and right thing."

"It didn't do no good."

"I guess you know now it is just as easy to do good as it is to do bad," he says.

I think of all those hooded men laughing. I think of all those men walking away from that fire, not catching any heat, no blame.

"No, it ain't," I finally say. "Doing good is harder. Doing nothing is the easiest of all."

Mr. Frank stays quiet and then nods. "You're right, Addy."

I bite my bottom lip. Even if I was right every day of my life, no one never ever, no one ever, told me so. It is hard *not* to smile and hug him, but we both, we just sit there a while longer on that log under which lay our buried map.

It is a school day the next day and we rise early like we have every day and Mr. Frank and I set out, same as we ever do, except that today we turn off and head toward the other schoolhouse. The burned-down schoolhouse.

When we get there, there's nothing left but a pile of burned-up mess.

Mr. Frank and me, we are not surprised or even awestruck by the destruction. We take it in like sleepwalkers and poke around some.

I look for the place where Jess Still had lain still. There is nothing on the ground to say that something terrible happened here. No blood, no bones, no markers or tombstones. Just this bad smell of burning.

There is not much left to do. There is not much more we can do.

I find a wood shingle that is not so burned from the fire and make the surface smooth. I think of what to cut on it with my pocketknife. How does a body ever know a person? I think on Jess Still and what I hear about him. Then I carve out and write what I do know.

I don't need Mr. Frank to assign me a theme. I write what needs to be said. Mr. Frank stands by me and he reads:

JESS STILL RISE
MURDERED AND KILLED
HERE
NOVEMBER 17, 1875

I bury that marker deep into the ground.

Chapter 7

Monday is washing day. I build a fire and carry water from the spring. I set the wash pot on the fire and dump all the clothes in, stirring in Mr. Frank's overalls and long-legged underwear with the troubling stick. I get the washboard and a cake of soap ready when Miss Irene comes outside and says for me to go on with Mr. Frank.

I am so glad, for I would much rather build a schoolhouse than wash clothes.

* * *

Most all of us schoolchildren come out to rebuild the schoolhouse with Mr. Frank. Most every able-bodied black man, and even a few white men, come to help build. Rew Smith and his pappy stay away.

Even the sheriff comes and starts the day with a little speech about how he and his men are trying to track down who did this and how it's important to let the law take care of things. Then we all pray some.

We have to haul lumber from a distance because the Yankees took out the sawmills.

Mostly we children haul lumber and help with the food for the men who are building. Some of the men are cutting the pine logs, peeling the bark, shaping them with a broadax, cutting V-shaped notches in both ends to make them ready to fasten together with wooden pegs. Early Rise and Mr. Frank's ma are in charge of the noontime meal. They have a wash pot over an open fire and they are sorting through all the foods women, black and white, bring in.

When we're all working together this way, the work goes fast.

Layer by layer, the log walls are rolled up and into place, notched and fitted at the corners. Mr. Frank cuts two stout young trees down entire and sets them up at both end walls, their branches trimmed into a crotch to support the ridgepole.

Near about lunchtime, Please Cook's son, Deuteronomy, blows an old cow horn.

We eat corn pone, greens, and turkey and dumplings. There are roasting ears, beans, and applesauce. It is still a bad time for folks. Money and goods is hard to come by, but there is game in the woods and here we all are eating up, all because we come together.

By the end of the first day, the chimney built out of mud and rocks is up. Deuteronomy calls it a "chimley."

Mr. Frank and the other men agree that this schoolhouse will have a wooden floor, not an earthen floor, and I volunteer to help haul off split logs for planks.

For a roof the men put on the bark slabs, laid like shingles and held in place by a log for weight. I can see they build the roof good, pulling a crosscut saw and toting the slab boards up on a ladder.

The town cannot afford glass windowpanes, so Mrs. Davenport paints some paper with hogs' lard to let in the light. In the summer, they can always knock out the clay between the logs for ventilation and light, then fill it in again in winter to keep out the cold.

At one side of each window is a kind of ornament resembling a doorknob for the purpose of holding curtains in place. Mrs. Davenport says that's the way they have it in her house, and she thinks children should feel special when they come to school.

At the end of the week, when everything is up and ready, Mr. Frank, he thinks to paint one wall in the room black so students can write on it with chalk and use pieces of cotton as erasers.

Then finally, Mr. Frank, he paints the ceiling a beautiful white.

"That's the prettiest thing I ever saw," I say, looking at the ceiling.

"We knew exactly what we wanted this time," Mr. Frank says. "That's one thing to be said for reconstructing."

When we are all through we stand back to admire our work.

"Is it OK to take pride in such a thing?" I ask.

Mr. Frank smiles. "In the Bible it says that in the beginning, each time God made something new, he stood back and said, 'It is good.' Now, *there* was a man proud of his work."

"'Cept he wasn't a man."

"Sometimes it helps to think of him as a man. To think of him as the grandpappy of us all."

I think on this some. I think until my brain starts itching again. What I don't understand is, where was the Lord Grandpappy that night the schoolhouse burned? What was he doing?

When we all finally do go back to school, Mrs. Davenport, she volunteers to teach us for the time when Mr. Frank goes away to New Orleans for supplies. When me and Miss Irene wave goodbye to Mr. Frank, I get a sinking feeling in the pit of my stomach. Pappy left and so did Momma. What makes me think Mr. Frank will come back?

A few mornings later, I go to the hen house like I always do, except this time I get this feeling something or someone is watching me. I hear a rustle, something slipping away. Is it a weasel? A possum? I hope not a fox.

In the coming light of the sun, I see a hand around a chicken's neck. I catch my breath and my eyes follow that hand up to an arm, and up further to the face of my pappy.

"Pappy?"

"Shhhh," he says.

It is Pappy, who didn't go to Texas after all, or is he back?

I walk over to him, not sure what I can or can't do. I put my hands on his arms, like the beginning of a hug he won't let me finish.

"Heh," he says, smiling. "That Frank Russell. He's gone, idn't he." Pappy lets go of the chicken's neck and I let go of him, glad to see the chicken clucking away again, going back to pecking around the hay for insects or corn.

"Pappy? You the one been stealin' them eggs and the chicken too?"

"I'm no chicken thief," he says, smiling, like he thinks it's funny. I cannot tell if he's joking. Is this another one of Pappy's pranks? "And I know you will not tell on me being here, because I am your pappy."

And he leaves. He just up and leaves, just like that, and I can't help but think and wonder, *Did this happen or was I dreaming?*

At noon I see Pappy coming down the road, heading straight our way. All these years of not seeing him. All the years I thought I forgot his face, and now he is becoming an everyday sight for me.

He tips his hat to Miss Irene. He looks to have cleaned himself up since this morning.

Miss Irene, she goes back into the house and I wonder what all she's doing. Getting a gun? I hear the china shake in the china cabinet as she hurries across the floor.

She comes out with some bills, goes to the edge of the porch, and bends down to hand them to Pappy, like she's petting a dog. Pappy looks at the bills and laughs until he coughs a bad-sounding cough.

"I don't want money, ma'am. I'm no beggar man. I come for my girl. You can't buy a person. Not nowadays, anyhow. Besides, this here is no legal tender. This here is Confederate monies." But he pockets it just the same because he and I both know you can get maybe ten cents for a ten-dollar Confederate bill.

I am sorry for Miss Irene then. She knows no better. She is alone, without her husband, and here in front of her is my mischievous pappy, a man people say has killed. She is thinking he is here because he wants money or food, here because he wants something from her. But I know he is here because of me. I have brought danger to poor Miss Irene's doorstep.

"Word is you and your husband plan on startin' a general store. With such dreadful men around, it behooves me to tell your husband to protect himself when he's going after supplies. And you being all alone here. You need to protect yourself too."

"Is that a threat, Mr. O'Donnell?"

"No threat at all. Just a fact. Dangerous times we live in." He spits tobacco juice off to the side, takes his hat off, and looks around some. "I come for Addy, Miss Russell. I'll finish the raising now, if you please."

Even from where I stand, I catch an oily smell on account of the grease he put in his hair to keep it back. He stands in the yard I swept clean and smooth, and he talks and holds his hat over the center of his chest. Miss Irene listens. Her eyes study him long and hard. I know she is taking in every last detail of what I see. Here stands a man come to reclaim his property.

He taught me how to catch lizards, kill ducks, feather chickens, skin rabbits. He taught me how to hold a gun and a knife. He taught me how to tree a possum, then how to shake him down. He taught me how to be a boy even though I was a girl. He taught me what Momma wouldn't, and how could I not feel a need to pay him back? When he looks me in the eye, I read what that look means to say. I seen that look before when he went calling on folks, getting them to pay up on bets he liked to make. His eyes are saying, *I come to collect.*

I can see that Miss Irene don't know what to do. This here's my pappy and he has a right to take me. And I bet she's wishing he'd just go on and do just that. Since I've been here, seems like nothing but trouble has come their way, just the way Mr. Frank thought it would be. Their eggs and chickens get stolen, a schoolhouse burned down and a little boy killed, and me, another mouth to feed. I take matters in my own two hands then and step down off the Russell porch.

Pappy, he hugs me, and when his beard scratches my face, I think of how Momma would have his hide on account of his scratchiness and ill-kept ways. He smells as though he has just been in the river where he bathes and I think that was for me. He cleaned up for me and I'm not used to this sorrowful feeling I have for Pappy, and I know right away that he wouldn't like it one bit—his twelve-year-old girl feeling sorry for him. No, he wouldn't like it one bit, and he'd surely whip me for that.

Pappy. He is bad and mean and dangerous, but he is still my pappy.

I think maybe it will be a fine thing to go back home, whatever is left of it, and sit in a familiar room among familiar things.

"Yer shoes is too big," he says, looking down at my feet. "I can fix those." I don't tell him Mr. Frank made me these shoes. I know he knows. Pappy, he knows everything.

I say my thank-yous and farewells to Miss Irene. Pappy won't let me take anything she wants to give. No blankets or biscuits or peaches. Nothing. We set to walking.

I look at the back of Pappy's slicked-back hair as he walks ahead of me to cross back into No-Bob. We don't say much because Pappy never did, not with me, anyway. But I can't help but wonder, *Did he go to Texas or was he here all along?*

He says, well, sure, he went off to Texas and to other places too.

"What were you gone so long for?"

He doesn't answer me. He tells me stories of his travels instead. He says he saw a woman with no legs or hands who cut out paper silhouettes by holding a common pair of scissors in her mouth. He says he met a man who sold skunk oil to people with rheumatism and another who could tell you your future by feeling the bumps on your head.

"Yeah?" I say. "What'd he say about you?"

He stops walking, turns around, and lays my hands on the top of his greasy head. I feel a few bumps and even a bald spot. I have my hands in Pappy's hair and I have to laugh and joke. "Which bump is it that makes a fellow a chicken thief?"

He sniffs through his nose. That's the way Pappy laughs. "I was meant to be a statesman," he says serious and proud, acting like a statesman, whatever that is. "I have natural ability."

I can't help but smile, and we walk on. Pines grow closer together out here at the edge of No-Bob where the road gets narrow and buggies can't pass easily. Breathing in the smell of the pine trees, poplars, and cypresses, taking in such beauty, you feel goodness. You don't want to be mean.

"Sure is pretty," I say, looking around, changing our line of talk.

I want to think that Pappy could love or at least that he could learn how to love. Maybe Mr. Frank or Miss Irene could teach him or maybe I could. But some folks don't have the learning in them. Some folks won't let their hearts open up for learning. That's what I've learned. I've learned that some people can learn and love both, and some people can't, and Pappy might very well be one of the can'ts.

Still, I feel hope for him.

We pass three goats. Pappy takes one of them and rubs snuff in its snout, then calls out to the farmer in the field and says, "Looka here." The farmer sees his goat snuffing and snorting and pawing at the ground.

"What's wrong with him?" the farmer asks.

"He's got a bad case of black snout," Pappy says.

"What's that?" the farmer asks.

"It's a catching sickness, and if you don't get rid of this one, the other two will get it for sure."

Pappy offers his services, saying for a peck of fruit wine or brandy he'll slaughter the goat himself, even dispose of him for the farmer. The farmer runs home and comes back with a peck of peach brandy, and Pappy leads the snuffing, snorting goat away.

"Come on, Addy Cakes," he says, chuckling to himself. "Better times coming."

Pappy used to call me Addy Cakes. *Addy Cake, Addy Cake, baker man,* he'd sing. *Bake me a cake as fast as you can. Pat it and prick it and mark it with an* A. *Put it in the oven for Addy and me!*

What else can I do but follow Pappy and the goat? This is not stealing because the farmer agreed. Tricking him is not the same as stealing. I say this to myself over and over, as though I am trying to talk myself into something.

When we get back home with the goat, there is no Momma

to hail us at the gate. From where I stand now, I see my house for what it is—a one-room frame hut leaning in a field of red clay.

"Where's Momma?"

"I was fixin' to ask you the same," Pappy says.

"She went to Texas to look for you."

He looks at me in a queer way as he thinks on this, then he laughs and laughs, though I don't know why.

"Did you go to Texas?" I ask.

"Sure I did," he says, not looking me in the eye.

Inside, the place does not look the same. We never did have much, no iron pot or fancy kitchen fireplace. No, here we cooked in a wash pot out in the yard over a fire with stakes on each side, with an iron bar across them to hang pots on. But Momma and I kept it clean and tidy when we lived here together.

Now it is a stale, sodden place, reeking of mud and garbage. The air is heavy with the smell of man sweat, whiskey, wet leather, and animal manure—cow and chicken both.

It's Pappy's place now. Pappy's old shirts, worn boots, empty bottles, and ripped breeches are on the floor, shoved aside in the corners. Rusted knives, bits of broken dishes, and chicken bones stick to the dirt floor.

It's winter now and he keeps the windows covered with wooden shutters. The flour sacks Momma put up for curtains are all tattered and half down. There are still two beds, but I don't know what happened to the table and chairs, and I know enough not to ask. The wind blows through the unfinished chinks in the sides of the house.

A barrel marked u.s. sits in one of the corners of the room. I break into it and see that it is filled with cornmeal. I set out to make cornbread. Pappy sees what I've done.

"How could you do such a thing?" he says. "That barrel of food wasn't meant for No-Bob, but for all of Smith County."

I look at him. He has half a grin starting to run across his mouth.

"That barrel was marked," I say. "It said 'U.S.,' so *us* commenced to eat from it."

Oh but Pappy sure likes this one. He repeats what I said himself. He slaps his leg. He says it over and over and he laughs and laughs as he slits the goat's neck.

That night, we feed all the O'Donnells who come by. Pappy says we are feasting to celebrate my homecoming. He tells everybody he sees about the cornmeal in the barrel marked u.s. He says, "See? What'd I tell you? She's one of our own."

I am proud that my pappy is so proud. We sit on the dirt floor eating goat meat, all around the open-pit fire inside a circle of stones.

Pappy brings out his fiddle and one of my uncles brings out his washboard and they play and we get up and dance the heel-and-toe and the forward-and-back, whirling and stomping across our bare earth floor.

There are plenty of greasy, smutty-faced O'Donnell children, some older, some younger than me, all of them—boys and girls—cussing like bad men. They smell like wet dogs and the dogs smell like them and the children don't care any more than the dogs do. Have O'Donnell children always been this dirty or am I just now seeing it? Was I like that? Am I going back to being like that, slipping back into old ways?

But it is good to see all of us O'Donnells whooping it up the way we can do, the way we used to do. These are my people. This is my family, my kin. Pappy calls us a clan. He says you can never run away from your people.

In the thick of the fun, Pappy introduces me to an O'Donnell who I know killed a man over a ten-cent bet in a game of cards. He goes by the name of Smasher. I don't know his real name.

Me and Smasher, we dance the two-step.

The tale of how Pappy got the goat is told again and again, all night long, with shouts of laughter and applause and "Black snout?" and "Tell it again, tell it again." All the while I'm thinking, *What of the farmer? What of the farmer's wife and children? What of the goat? When is a good story not nice? When does funny turn into just plain mean?*

I do feel sorrowful bad for that farmer, as dumb as he was. But I am powerful hungry and I can't think but to eat.

Pappy, he drinks a might too much moonshine. He lies across a bed, turns weepy, and says he doesn't have but five cents to his name, and he runs his hand in his pocket and pulls out a silver dollar and says, "Where did I get that?"

I tap him on the shoulder and say, "You got it out of your pocket, Pappy." I think everyone is happy. I tell him to put it back in his pocket and he puts it back in his pocket.

"You don't want to be here," he says to me, his voice going hard and angry all at once.

"You're wrong, Pappy."

He turns to Smasher and says, "I won't let my girl go in any house in this county but yours."

"You need to eat some, Pappy."

"You," Pappy says, turning to me. I look at his face and I back away quick. "You don't tell me what to do. You will do as you are told. I am your pappy, all right." He gets up as if to leave but recalls it is his house. He pulls out his knife and looks at me. Everybody goes quiet.

This is what always happens—every Saturday the men meet up, stand around, drink, spit, and insult one another until the fighting starts.

I give Pappy his fiddle. He looks at his knife in one hand and the fiddle in his other.

"Go on and play something, Pappy," I say.

Pappy starts to play.

Late that night I am half-asleep, listening to the slow, low talk of Smasher and the other O'Donnell men around the burning and crackling fire, Pappy sharpening his knife with a rock he always carries in his pocket.

I listen to them recounting Pappy's exploits, how he used to fight so long and so hard that the fighters had to stop and use a pocketknife to pick the knuckle skin from between their teeth, how Pappy tied up that man to a plow as though he were a mule and made him plow a field.

"Wadn't that man your brother Garner?"

And they all laugh even harder.

Somebody says something that sounds like *Addy knows too much.* Then I hear Pappy say, "Addy?"—not *to* me but *about* me.

"Yer wrong," he says. "Even if she knew, Addy would never betray her pappy. 'Member—she's an O'Donnell first and foremost. She's loyal."

I fall asleep thinking how I *am* loyal and how now, out of the blue, I want to prove that to Pappy.

That night I dream that all the women in No-Bob have bird beaks for noses and walk around with their beaks in the air, squatting every now and then to peck at their children. The men all have monkey faces that they try to pull off but can't.

I wake up in a sweat, and when I get up to splash my face, the water in the washing pot inside has frozen and I almost break my knuckles breaking the ice to get to the water.

At dawn I do what I did for Mr. Frank and Miss Irene. I draw water from the well, kindle the fire, cook up some cornbread. I set to sweeping the dirt floor, thinking now that I know what a real house looks like, I can fix this broken-up one. Now that I have helped build a school, I can rebuild this here house.

Pappy sleeps all morning and arises to dress at noon, tucking his knife and pistol into his pants. It's like he's not dressed without his knife and pistol.

"Come on," he says. "You, me, we got a meeting with Smasher."

Chapter 8

I am to marry Smasher.

Pappy tells me this on the way to Smasher's house while he teaches me some about the stars and such, even though it is still day. He tells me about the night the stars fell. He says he doesn't know where the stars go when they fall from the sky. They just fall and go out, not hurting nobody.

Then he complains about the quiet all around us. He says he thinks better with a lot of noise, noise like screaming and yelling, gunfire and shouting. The silence irks him, but the quiet is what I like.

"I don't want to marry Smasher," I whisper.

He stops and looks at me square on. "You *will* marry Smasher. And if you don't, I'll throw yer hide to the snakes in the swamp."

Pappy says the Bible says to "multiply and replenish the earth" and his pappy took that part of the Bible real serious because he set out to do just that and had twenty-two children with two different wives. Pappy doesn't say "at the same time," but I know that to be true too.

"I don't want to marry nobody, Pappy. I'm not but twelve years old. I can live with you, cook and clean for you. I want to be with you and go back to the schoolhouse and learn some more." I wished I brought my blue-back speller with me. I'd only got as far as *baker* in it.

"Mr. Frank says—"

Pappy swings around and puts his hand over my mouth so that I cannot speak. His hand smells of tobacco.

"I never ever want to hear you say that name again, you hear?" He takes his hand away from my mouth. "Everything that Frank and Irene said to you? Forget. Forget it all."

I stare down at my shoes. "Yes, sir."

He palms the asafetida bag I wear around my neck. Then he yanks it off and throws it to the ground.

"Us O'Donnells, we don't wear these either," he says, turning to walk on.

Without him seeing, I pick the bag from the dirt and stuff it in my pocket.

"You think you so smart now you read and write. Well. Guess what, you're thirteen. You missed a birthday. And besides, you've had enough schooling. I'll school you from here on out. Schoolhouse or no schoolhouse, you'll never be as smart as your pappy. Never."

What would Momma tell me? What would she have me do? Would she want me marrying Smasher? All that time, living with Momma, I missed Pappy. All that time. Now here I am living with Pappy and I'm missing missing missing my momma.

We walk a ways up the trail. A peddler stops to ask me to fasten the trace that has come loose on his wagon. I fasten the trace, but Pappy pulls the peddler out of his wagon.

"She don't do what *anybody* tells her," Pappy says to the man, putting his face in his face. "She does what *I* tell her." Pappy slaps the man, cuts his shirttails off, and tells him to drive on before he cuts him good.

We watch the peddler drive off, fast. I know I should feel bad for that peddler, but I am proud and confused that Pappy took up for me. I don't do what *anybody* tells me. I do what Pappy tells me.

It is Saturday and Smasher hails us at the gate and invites us in. The pine groves grow almost to his door. He lives in a one-room place just like ours with his twin brother, Eustace.

Straight away we sit down to eat. On their round kitchen table is a contraption, a wheel that you put the food on and it goes around and around so others can get at the food and nobody has to serve you. Smasher calls the wheel his "lazy wife."

Pappy sits me next to Smasher. Smasher, he still has both his ears but he has a rising smell. He has slicked back his hair and waxed his mustache, but he needs to bathe.

I think about how Miss Irene might suggest Smasher have a bath by fetching him some soap and water, and just thinking of her again makes me smile. My smiling makes Smasher smile and gets him started talking about how so many people died in the war. He talks about the difference between dying and getting killed. How getting killed was better than just dying. He thinks he's being entertaining.

Eustace says nothing. He just chews with his mouth open and stares at me.

Pappy tells the story about the peddler we passed and he makes them laugh.

We eat cornbread and field peas somebody boiled good and soft.

Pappy feels inclined to tell us all again how No-Bob came to be.

It all started when Pappy's pa, Pappy O'Donnell, moved to this part of the country and settled and acquired a good bit of land cheap because the land flooded from the rivers when the rains came. People said the land was of inferior quality, only good for livestock, but that's why Pappy O'Donnell liked it. He said there won't ever be none of those big plantations nearby because nobody would want to live here—the rest of the world would leave us alone.

He raised a might large family. Some say he had twenty-two children, some say twenty-eight. He tried to give all his children a home, and each of them married into another family, and that's when the bad name was given over to the O'Donnells because there was so much feuding over the dividing of the property. Pappy said they wanted to keep the land pure and full of white, Anglo-Saxon O'Donnells.

A spider comes down on a single strand just to say hey. She's swinging in the breeze, happy just to be hanging there, when Pappy says, "Swat it down and step on it."

I don't want to smash the spider. I look at it and whisper to it, "Get."

Pappy comes round the table, swats the spider down, lifts his foot, then looks me in the eye when he stomps down on that spider, and I can't look at the mess on the floor.

The men all wink at each other as they pass around the jug. Pappy drinks from the jug and then he makes a face. Why does he keep drinking that stuff when I know he doesn't like it?

We hear a horse's hoofs with the muffled sound they have clattering across the road. Then we hear the thud of a wooden leg on the front porch.

It is Mr. Smith. He eyes me as he sits down at the table with us. They all four of them do some special handshake and greeting. I can't help but think that it looks to be such foolish, childish business.

Mr. Smith brings news that the sheriff of Raleigh has put out a warrant for his arrest. He stops and looks at Pappy. "They want to arrest you too, Mark. They want the both of us because we are the primary suspects. That's what they say. They won't let this one go."

"What fer?" Smasher asks.

"Burning the schoolhouse that killed that little darky," Mr.

Smith says. "Word in town is folks is sick of all the violence against the darkies. Sheriff is getting pressure from higher-ups." Mr. Smith smiles and says it seems that lynching and brutality has spread all over the state. Smasher laughs and Eustace claps his hands. Mr. Smith goes on to say that he heard that the governor of Mississippi telegraphed President Grant for assistance, only to be told that Mississippi had to take care of its own affairs.

We all look at Pappy, who hasn't said a thing. A long long time ago, Pappy made up his mind he would never go to jail, not ever. He has spent many a night hiding out in Cohay swamp.

He pats my hand. "Don't you worry none, Addy Cakes."

The law's got it wrong. Pappy is bad, but he is not that bad.

He starts to smile. My pappy? He smiles when he's angry, laughs when he fights.

"Well. They gonna have to come get me first. And then, they gonna have to find me." The three of them all have a good laugh, all excepting Pappy.

I hear Mr. Smith whisper to Pappy something about Mr. Frank. I hear him say, "And he's headed home again." Pappy winks at me as if I'm in on it with them.

"Smasher, let's us take care of business before we settle the wedding arrangements," Pappy says.

Smasher looks at me, then nods his head. "All right then."

They drink from the jug and make more faces.

"We'll break him up some," Mr. Smith says. I look at him and think about what his son, Rew Smith, said to me a while back in the schoolyard. He said he wouldn't play with an O'Donnell. He said his pa told him not to. He said his pa said the O'Donnells got the devil in them. Said I was part black myself. This Smith boy, Rew. He would not drink milk after me.

So why is this Mr. Smith sitting down now to eat and drink with the devils?

Mr. Smith takes the jug and drinks after Pappy.

"Christmas is a-coming," Pappy says.

I have such dark winter feelings. I wish it was spring.

Mr. Smith stays the night with Pappy and me, staying low, he says, and the following morning, Pappy goes away all of a sudden with Mr. Smith, Smasher, and Eustace. I sweep the house clean for Christmas. I may have missed my birthday, but I will not miss Christmas. I cut pine and magnolia branches and bring them into the house, hang them over the windows, and lay some on the table. I put pine branches in a jar full of water on the floor and the room smells up sweet and nice.

They come back not but a day later and cover our table

with goods from New Orleans—apples, figs, bananas, pineapples, bolted calico, bullet molds, cutlery, tinware, cooking pots, white flour, and two coconuts. We even have so much coffee, Pappy says he'll drink it now with every meal. Where did he get all this coffee after so many years when we made coffee with dried pea pods, roasted acorns, and once, Momma even sifted the bran from cornmeal to cook it to make coffee?

Pappy does not take notice of the cut branches.

I stare at the bounty on our table. Pappy takes the saber he used on the battlefields that's hanging on the wall, and with it, he cuts one of those coconuts in two, clean and smooth.

"Merry Christmas," he says, giving me half the coconut. "Now go bake us a cake." He joins up with the others and they all ride out, talking loud about where to get hold of some moonshine.

I set out trying to recall how Momma once made a coconut cake, starting with the flour, then the eggs, thinking all the while that it takes almost a week to get to New Orleans and back.

I am frosting a good-looking cake when who comes in through the door but Mr. Frank, the day's sunlight lit up behind his head. His right eye is black but he is smiling to see me, and I rush to him and hug him tight.

"How you doin', Addy?" he whispers.

"Tolerable well," I whisper back.

We break away so we can have a look at each other.

"Miss Irene told me where to find you."

"What happened to your eye?" I ask.

"Never mind about that," he says.

"That happen in New Orleans?"

"New Orleans is grand, Addy. You would love it." He tells me about the plank sidewalks there and the women's fancy hairstyles, their hair threaded with gold ropes and embroidered ribbons such as he's never seen. His left eye is still bright with the city. I imagine that even the soles of his shoes still smell of the trampled fruit from a New Orleans marketplace.

"I wanted to give you these." Mr. Frank, he holds up a pair of store-bought shoes. Not girl shoes that dig into my ankles, like he made me. These here are boy shoes. Work shoes already made soft. Walking shoes. Running shoes. I put them on my feet and my feet are yelling out their thank-yous. I join up with them. These here store-bought boy shoes are my first comfortable shoes.

I say, "Oh, oh, oh." And when I look at him, his one eye is watering.

"And Miss Irene, she wanted me to give you these." He

hands over a jar of peaches from his ma's pantry and a coat, a good, blue wool coat that fits me just right. Not too small, but still big enough for me to grow into.

"Merry Christmas, Addy."

I look into Mr. Frank's one watering eye and think how far he and me have both come. He used to hate O'Donnells. I can't forget that. He said we were "self-willed" and "haughty." He said we were "undisciplined" and "filthy." He said words I know the meanings of now. I don't know when that changed and I don't care to know. All I know is that he looks at me differently now. It takes a little bit of bravery to change your way of thinking about people, and I can't help but ponder: Would other people change like Mr. Frank? Could Pappy? Could I?

"I sure wish I had some little something to give you, Mr. Frank," I say, looking around the room.

"Being right here's enough."

Maybe someday I can do something for Mr. Frank. Maybe someday he'll even ask.

I think about their Christmas and mine. I think how nice it would have been to wake up in Mr. Frank's fine house that morning, light a fire, milk the cow, open a present, and be with them both.

"What did you bring back Miss Irene?"

He lowers his head and says, "Just a few things. Some calico and coconuts."

I always have been slow. This I know. But right now, I want to hurl that beautiful coconut cake outside the door.

"What happened, Mr. Frank?" I am just barely whispering.

"It's none of your concern, Addy. It was just another robbery. Happens a lot nowadays."

"How many of 'em?"

He looks at me square. "Four."

The two of us, we sit there, knowing what we know.

"Mr. Frank? Did you want to grow up and be like your pa?"

Mr. Frank, he sits and thinks on that. "I wanted to be like everyone else but me. I wanted to be like my brother, my pa, and my grandpa." He smiles kindly at me. "But you see, I was wrong to want that. You become who you were meant to become, and you can spend a lifetime trying to figure out who you were meant to become."

I nod, pretending I understand what all he's talking about. "I love my pappy," I say, thinking, pondering, itching my head. "It makes me terrible sick that I don't like him."

"I reckon I gotta shoot your eyes out when I see you." It is Pappy's dark shape standing there at the door, and from the sound of his voice, I know he has found moonshine. He staggers in and slaps Mr. Frank on the back. "By ginger, have a drink with me, Shanks."

"I don't drink."

"That's not what I hear."

"I best be going."

"Leaving No-Bob? So soon?" Pappy eyeballs him up and down.

"You don't need to come here starting fights, Mr. O'Donnell."

"I don't start fights, mister. I finish them."

"He came to visit with me, Pappy. He is our guest."

"I came here to see Addy. I didn't come here to fetch anything that is mine." Mr. Frank is looking at all the bounty.

I am glad when Pappy yawns. That means he is all out of ideas and mischief. I give Mr. Frank a little push on the arm. I whisper, "Leave now."

Mr. Frank leaves on his horse and Pappy swipes his finger across the top of the cake, licking the icing, while I watch Mr. Frank ride away.

I hear something break and I turn around to see my jar of pine branches broken on the floor. Pappy screams and curses, saying I should know by now how much he hates anything from the outside inside. He never wants to see pine branches or flowers inside his house again, and he sure doesn't want them or anything like them on his grave. I don't say it, but I think it: *Pappy will never have to worry about somebody putting flowers on his grave.*

That night all the O'Donnells come round for a big frolic and all the men come in sweaty, bragging loud and jostling each other. They greet each other with some special, silly handshake, making up words starting with *kl,* like *klavern, kleagle, kluupa,* and *klonvocation.* And they say all this with their low, serious voices and I can hardly stop myself from laughing out loud.

The women are quiet and set to work. They know to do just that, stay low and quiet. All the O'Donnell women are bony and quiet, their hair pulled back in tight buns and their thin lips set to stay shut. You don't see them smile much. They do not speak because they know not to. More than a few of them have black eyes from the night before, when they might have spoken out of turn.

Hams, turkey, chicken, all sorts of jam and jellies, come out from people's smokehouses and cellars; berry pie, buttermilk, and hot corn pone, and I keep thinking, *Where was all this fine food when me and Momma were so hungry?* The men eat first and the boys and girls fill in, then the women eat last while the children get dusty wrestling and playing leapfrog.

Smasher wishes me a happy Saturday. He says "Satidy." He hands me over a bunch of wildflowers in a jar, which I put away in the smokehouse, not in Pappy's house.

"Addy?" Smasher says to me. His breath smells of moonshine and he still hasn't bathed. But there's a sweetness to him, a sweetness I imagine Momma saw in Pappy. "Why you go and put my flowers in the smokehouse, Addy? Why you bein' so mean to me?"

"Never you mind, Smasher. Go on. I'm busy."

He puts both his hands on my shoulders and smashes his dried-out lips into mine. He smashes so hard I can feel his two front teeth. He steps away, smiling. Now I know how he got his name.

"If you ain't the blessedest," he says, smiling, showing his dirty, brown teeth.

And this is my first kiss. From Smasher. And all I feel like doing now is washing my mouth out with soap.

"I told you to wait," Pappy says. "I suppose now I gotta knock all your teeth out."

Smasher thinks Pappy is kidding, but I can see by his face that he is not. I can smell Pappy's anger and it smells like a fish coming out of a fire.

"Ah, Smasher," I say. "What you need teeth for, anyway?" I say.

He waits and thinks on this. "To chew," he says.

"No," I say. "To keep your gums from sticking together."

It takes both Pappy and Smasher a minute, but when they laugh, they clap their hands together and then slap each other's backs. Oh but they like that one. I back away, relieved they aren't fighting.

Pappy brings out his fiddle, and Eustace, who usually never says a word, calls out, "Hoedown!" and fixes to call out the dances loud and clear. Soon enough the menfolk, married and single, are slinging the single women around, dancing and having themselves a big time. Most of the married women clean up or stand against the walls and watch. Some clap their hands and stomp along. They are careful not to dance with anyone but their husbands, for to do otherwise will start a fight.

Everybody loves my coconut cake, but I can't eat a bite. Everywhere I look is O'Donnell, O'Donnell, O'Donnell.

* * *

That night around the fire, I listen to Pappy and the other men talk. It all comes out in stories meant to be funny, meant to make people laugh. There is the story about the black man who didn't tip his hat as he passed and the white man who killed him, put him in a hollow log, and sunk his body in the swamp. There is the story about the black man they dragged out of bed only to beat out his eyes with corncobs. There is story after story, each one more embroidered, stories of torture and killing, stories of white men pestering black men, white men pestering Indians, and at the end of each telling, there is some punch line or twist that makes the white man win, and everybody laughs, relieved.

When I was in the kitchen with the women, or outside stirring a pot, I used to love listening to women talk. Momma would tell somebody how to make a tea or a salve. Somebody else would tell how someone was cured or saved. I used to love their hear-tell. But our men's stories are different. They talk about how people get hurt.

"Gimme that," a girl says to her little sister. She takes a ball from out of her hand and the little girl starts crying. Their mother slaps the crying girl on the head. The sister with the ball laughs and sticks her tongue out.

I look around at all the other women and children at the fire, listening to the stories their men tell. And I can't help but think that the children in No-Bob turn out just as mean as their mommas and pappies because this is where they learn all about mean.

Maybe Mr. Frank was right the first time about all of us O'Donnells. Mean just makes more mean.

Finally, Pappy tells his story of thieving Mr. Frank and it is told all night again and again, each time the laughter rising louder and louder when Pappy says low and serious, "You know, they used to call him 'Shanks.'" And that gets everybody laughing even louder and I can't do a thing about any of it.

After all the fun and carrying on, and after all the women and children leave, the men stay behind and Pappy's talk turns serious. He talks about what a terrible, sorrowful job Ulysses Grant is doing in Washington and how ex-Confederates have to work hard to get their vote back, seeing how they are now banned from voting. He says it's not right to fight and fight for your country, then come home and not be able to vote. He *says* he wishes he'd never seen the violence and slaughter he saw at the Battle of Franklin, but to hear him tell it, I'm not so sure. For five hours his commander charged his soldiers to move forward. Seventeen hundred and fifty of them killed, 3,800 wounded, 702 missing. "My flesh trembles when I think of it. Would to God that I never witnessed such a scene."

We hear a screech owl.

In the Bloody Angle area at Spotsylvania, Pappy says he and his repelled thousands of charging Yankees at Fort Gregg, throwing rocks when ammunition gave out. Some of them even went with Robert E. Lee when he surrendered at Appomattox. They called themselves the Smith County Defenders because they weren't fighting for anything—they were defending.

"So tell me," Pappy says. "We come home, broken, and we're supposed to stand aside and watch those colored boys vote while we can't?"

I stay down low under my quilt, and as I listen I think, *How much of this meanness I see now started with warring? How much of all these everyday violent ways began with battlefield battles?* Mr. Smith, Pappy, and so many other men were paid and taught to kill for a cause, then they lost and they were supposed to go home peaceful, legally bound now to a new united country. Wasn't that asking too much? Who thought of these rules?

"I'm glad Grant said for Mississippi to work it out. I don't want no government handouts," Pappy says.

"The Klan don't have no use for the carpetbaggers and scallywags making the rules," somebody says. "Don't have no use for them no way."

"You hear that fellow from Maine is planning to run for governor of Mississippi? What's his name, Ames?" Pappy says.

I hear, "Jesus God Almighty."

"They look down on us; all of them do up north," Pappy says. "But I tell you what. I'd rather be somebody's enemy than someone's loser. Course, I'd rather be neither. I'd rather just be Mark O'Donnell, only better off, but how am I supposed to do that?" He stares at the fire, thinking on the circle he just talked himself into. His face is filled with furrows and canals where dirt has caked in. He still parts his hair down the middle, but that's only when he parts his hair. Tonight it's slicked back, then thrown off to both sides helter-skelter. His ears poke out uneven and his chin has a cleft that Momma always liked. The worry lines across Pappy's forehead look like all the rivers running in these parts, rivers that don't ever meet up and don't ever seem to end.

When I wake up before the sun, I put on my new store-bought boy shoes and carefully, quietly step over all the sleeping men. The room smells like man feet and man breath. I don't see

Pappy, but I do see Smasher, who is asleep and snoring on his back with his mouth open, a line of spittle running into a puddle on the ground.

I stop when I see one man sleeping in a hood-and-mask costume. I walk around this still figure, lying sprawled out and asleep on the ground. I recognize the hood and then the hood's mask. It is the fancy hood with the extra slits above the eyes, mouth, and nose, like worry lines, that belonged to the man who lit the match that lit the cross that fell on the colored schoolhouse and burned it down and killed Jess Still.

I stand still for a very long time, looking down, staring at this person covered in a sheet with the mask. I do not have to pull off the mask to know who this is, but I do. I have to. I do it carefully. I bend down. I take the ends in my fingers, and quietly, gently, I lift the hood from the sleeping head it covers. Without thinking, I ball up the hood in my fists and stuff it in my pocket.

When I see him, when I recognize for sure that this here is my own pappy, I cannot say that I am surprised, but for a minute I cannot breathe. He does not wake up. He sleeps on like a baby. What could he be dreaming?

I think, *Now it is worse because the killers are not only just men, one of them is my pappy.* If they were monsters, we would just get rid of them and not think twice. But they are men. They are our men. They are one of us. They are who we are. And him? He is my pappy. He is who I am.

Pappy, who people say is such a jokester in No-Bob. My pappy, who lives to make people laugh. It was Pappy who burned a cross over thirty feet high in front of the colored people's church. It was Pappy who killed my sweet little friend named Jess Still.

Last night they said they were curing what they called the horrors of anarchy and reckless Negro rule. But Pappy and these O'Donnell men? These men are stirring up a fight when there is no fight. These men, this whole nation of men, were forced to quit the war in 1865, when they lost. Then they got mad and started to fight each other. They are trying to make it so that it is like it was before all the fighting and they kill anybody and everybody who disagrees.

I put together what I've known all along but couldn't admit to myself. I think of the talk last night, what Pappy said, the secret handshakes. All around me are my people. All around me are violent men, killers, members of the Klan. I could run and tell Mr. Frank now so he could get the sheriff who has the warrant for Pappy's arrest, but I think, *No, I cannot, should not.* Already I have brought too much trouble to the Russell home.

I look down at my sleeping pappy. If I could, I would shake him awake this instant and stand before him and tell it to his face. I would say to him, *Pappy? You are a killer and a thief. You have stolen so much from so many. You have taken lives. You will not steal from me. You will not steal away my life.* But I could never say this to his face.

I look around at all the passed-out, sleeping men in this grungy one-room house, and it's like seeing the map in Mr. Frank's schoolhouse for the first time. I see exactly where I am now, and I know what to do. I do just what Pappy would do if he were his own little girl. I bundle up some leftover cornbread and sweet potatoes in my quilt. I put on my new blue coat and tie the quilt around me so the food won't fall out. I take the asafetida bag from my pocket and hang it around my neck.

Then I step over everybody laying there on the ground and I keep stepping and stepping and stepping until I am running. And I keep running. I only have one plan and that plan is to get out.

You have to cross No-Bob to cross out of No-Bob and I do. I run across No-Bob and away into the piny woods where the trees sway like dancers and the hills are snakes curling their backs.

Chapter 9

Once in the woods, I walk the paths that few know, past misty fields sprayed with leftover, worn-out corn and rows of longleaf pines standing soldier straight. I say hey to the frogs and the rabbits and the birds and Mr. Snake who slithers into some sunshine to sun himself.

When I need to do my business, I squat in the field like a partridge.

I keep moving to stay warm. I walk further away from the roads, to where the pines grow closer together, to where horses can't pass through. I am grateful for the shoes and the good, warm coat Mr. Frank gave me. Did he know? Did he know how I would need and use them both? I only wish I'd taken the jar of peaches. No peaches better than the ones from those two trees in front of Little Bit's house. Little Bit and Jack are two lucky people, to have all the fried chicken and peaches they can eat. Do they know their own good fortune?

No-Bob is not but six miles long and three miles wide, but who's to say really where it starts and stops?

I need to get far away from No-Bob. I set out for my very own forty days and forty nights.

I walk and walk and walk some more, and when night comes, I set up camp along Leaf River. It has warmed up some, and my coat is hot and heavy. I take it off, then my shoes and all the rest. I think to use the white sand along the shore to scrub my body clean. Then I plop myself all the way into the river and bathe myself. I've walked so far and I am so dirty, the icy water feels good and clean. I think about Little Bit then, how she said she was baptized and her ma was baptized in, where was it, Magnolia? I look around at all the trees and name the ones I know. Papaw, black tupelo, sweet gum, sassafras. I wish I had some other words to say, because this here bathing is not like any other. Maybe it is the cold water. Maybe it is this here river and the black, wet, sweet-smelling land all around me. Or maybe it is because I have run away.

Lord, I say. *I am very much alone right now. Would you mind please holding my hand?*

It is quiet, like church before the O'Donnells come in, prop their guns up in the corner against the back wall, then praise and sing. The moon is high in the sky, full and bright, and if it could make a sound, it would sound like moths in a lantern trying to get out.

I bundle up in my coat and quilt and make a bed of dried leaves so that I am not sleeping on the cold ground. As it gets darker, I hear panthers screaming way off in the forest and the wildcats howling and now I miss miss miss Momma and Pappy and I think, *How did I ever get into this pickle?*

This land? This land is just barely tame, and I think, *What am I doing in it?* You can't ever tame it. You can't grab a hold of this land. It grabs a hold of you. I tell myself I know these woods as good as any, but even I have to admit I picked the wrong time of year to leave shelter. I think to stay here only as long as it takes for me to think up another plan.

The trees look like they're cut out from black paper against the sky, and the sound of wind rustling through cane is like no other. It's not a happy sound, not like the rustle of a woman's petticoat, nor is it lonely like the *swoosh* going through the tops of longleaf pines. It's mournful-like. Wishful, like maybe someone's out there calling for you, and you know it's the wrong thing to do to get up and go toward that sound, but still, you want to.

I look up and wonder if the stars will fall tonight, the way they did back when Pappy was a young man. He said that the night he saw stars fall, they didn't fall on anyone and they didn't hurt nobody, but nobody knew where they went. Maybe they fall through the cracks in the ground. Maybe they land in the streams and ponds where the water puts them out.

When Momma shut me up in the chifforobe and I rubbed my eyes with my knees, I saw pictures behind my eyelids and counted the stars inside my mind. Now I can see them with my eyes wide open, right in front of me up there in the sky. And even though I don't know everything there is to know about stars, and I don't know what will or will not hurt me, I am not so scared anymore because I am glad I am out of the chifforobe.

I fall asleep thinking on those falling stars.

* * *

The next day I walk on, deeper into the forest, across Leaf River. I pick up a good stick and make a notch in it for the day I've been gone.

I stand before the hackberry tree on Fisher Creek. This is the tree that is supposed to have water dripping from its branches and leaves. Momma told me the legend of an Indian maiden named Onumbee, or "Gentle South Wind."

Onumbee's lover was sent forth into war. Every day Onumbee went to a place to wait for the return of her love, watching for him day after day, hoping he would make his way back. The lover never returned, and, supposing he was killed, she began pining away. She finally died of a broken heart and was buried at the place where she waited and watched. All that remains is a hackberry tree, which is said to have water continually dripping from its branches and leaves. The drops of water are the tears shed by Onumbee, still crying because her soul still waits at the lookout for her lover.

I think now that Momma got her missing ideas from the story of Onumbee.

Or is this the hackberry tree where Mr. Sanders tied his pregnant slave woman and whipped her until she died, and everybody knew that when you went around that tree, you could hear that baby cry?

I am tired, but I will not sit under that hackberry tree to rest. All around me the place is hard and gray, stained with yellow-brown, and it is cold and lonely and the wind moves through the trees, moaning and moaning, groaning and whistling.

I stare down at the river. I think of that slave that Mr. Russell once owned. Buck was his name. Little Bit told me a little bit about him. Mr. Frank and his pa walked him to the river Strong and Mr. Russell gave him a pair of eyeglasses and his freedom papers. Then Buck crossed the river all by himself, even though he was scared of water. He did it. He crossed over.

I touch the asafetida bag around my neck and move on, turning my pockets inside out to stop death. I head west toward Oakohay Creek, where I head north toward Cohay swamp. The woods is quiet and mournful. I stay away from canebrakes because of the wildcats.

By Hatchapaloo Creek I stumble on a bone so sharp, it cuts my leg. The bone is a leg bone. A big man's bone and it lies on top of more bones, all of them leg bones or arm bones. I recognize a torn piece of Confederate uniform, and then another piece from a Federal uniform. I look all around me and see that I'm standing in a shallow grave full of bones from severed limbs, bones of our men on both sides, pappies, sons, grandpappies, brothers, and husbands. Not North or South bones, nor black, red, or white bones. Not even bones from a good family or a bad family. Just bones. Cut-off, sawed-off limbs turned into cut-off, sawed-off bones. All of them the same color now.

The bones do not scare me. I have cut up too many chickens and seen one too many hog killings to be afraid of a few leg bones. *I'm sorry,* I say to the bones. I'm sorry you are separated from your masters. I'm sorry I am stepping over you.

And I move on.

I find a cave guarded by trees, some of them maple, magnolia, some birch, some I don't know the names of. I don't find any bear or human being inside the cave. I heard tell about a Negro man who escaped his plantation and hid out in a cave all during the war. Last I heard, though, he was still there, telling people it was not time to come out yet. His people weren't hardly free.

Right in front of the cave, on the black dirt along the river, I crouch down and soak my cut leg in the water. While I'm down there, I catch a fish with a stick, and I eat that fish whole, cooked at a fire I build. For dessert, there are dried huckleberries and chestnuts. I sit by the water, sucking on a cold, ripe, smushy persimmon, thinking nobody has to cook this into anything to make it good.

Away from the water, I collect spider webs to put over my cut and I wrap it with mud and sit awhile until it dries.

On this night, I sleep so well and warm inside the cave, I could be a bear and sleep there through the winter. I dream that I get up in this cave, and there next to me is a tiny man with twigs and leaves in his long hair. He says he has a gift for me and I am to choose one. He holds out a knife, some bright, black berries, and some roots. I already have a pocketknife. The berries I know are poison nightshade, and the root is from a sassafras tree. I choose the root because I like sassafras tea and I know how to make it.

When I wake up, I am so sure that the little man is there in the cave with me, I look all over for him. My fire is burned out, but the coals are still bright embers, and the air smells of vanilla. In my hand, I'm holding a chunk of sassafras root.

Outside the cave, all I see are acres and acres of these long-leaf pines run through with rivers. I get water and set to making sassafras tea by the fire, and I decide to make camp here in this cave for as long as I need to.

* * *

I count the notches in the stick I carry in my coat pocket. Nine. Nine days of eating the fish I catch and the nuts I find, the berries and persimmons, sharpening my knife with the stone I keep in my pocket, and sleeping in the cave where I dream almost every night of the little man, and each night, he offers me the gifts. Sometimes the little man offers me a gun instead of a knife. Or he offers me poison oak or jimsonweed, but every night I pick the root or the herbs, knowing in my dream mind that I can use them to make something to help me or somebody else.

During the day, I explore the riverbanks and learn the rivers, remembering the names and what all I seen on the map in Mr. Frank's schoolhouse. Oakohay Creek flows from its source on the Smith–Scott county line and empties into Leaf. Big and Little Hatchapaloo run into Oakohay. The Leaf and Chickasawhay form the Pascagoula River that empties into Pascagoula Bay. The Pearl River, with its tributaries the Strong and the Bogue Chitto, empties into the Gulf of Mexico. All of these waters are streams or tributaries and they are never stagnant and they don't dry up. Now I know why Mr. Frank says if a river forgets its source, it dries up.

What happens to a person who leaves her family, her

source? When I lived with Mr. Frank and Miss Irene, *I* didn't dry up and die.

Every now and then, I go back to the land of the bones by Hatchapaloo Creek and say some words. *I'm so sorry,* I say. *I'm real sorry.*

I miss people and I don't. I miss eating with people. I miss the smell of Momma and even Pappy, but not Smasher. I miss hearing Mr. Frank's steady voice and sitting next to him on his praying log. I miss his questions and everyday concerns. I miss the kind softness of Miss Irene, and the sound of her voice and her lady-laugh. I miss them both asking, "How are you today, Addy?" every morning, like they really wanted to know, and always waiting for my answer. And I wish more than anything I could just play here in the cave and in the water with Little Bit and Jess Still.

I can barely remember what Momma looks like. What was her first name again? What would she say to me being alone in the woods for so long? What would she have me do?

At night I feel Momma asking after me. *Addy? What have you gotten yourself into now?* Off a ways, I hear the water from the Hatchapaloo falling and joining up with the Oakohay.

I think on all the pioneers and outlaws that come before me, most all men, who lived in the wilderness, surviving by sleeping in caves or a hollow tree or even, if need be, inside the carcass of a bear to stay warm.

One night I hear people coming on horseback, and I know from the sounds of their voices that it's Mr. Smith and his men who have traveled some distance to get all the way out here. For what, I do not know.

I stamp out my fire, leave my cave, and, crouching under the canebrake, I watch.

A whole army passes, all of them with hoods and cut-out scare-faces on, heading toward Hatchapaloo Creek. It is like the war is starting all over again, and this here is a ghost army. More military-like than the real military, because during the war, most our soldiers didn't even have uniforms or horses. They were just ragtag units out to defend what they thought was theirs when all along this land belonged to nobody, North or South. This land, it is of itself.

I even think that I hear the sound of Pappy's voice. Then I hear the fearful, sad cries of someone they have, someone they are hurting.

I run and follow, trying to stay close behind, using the canebrakes as cover and shortcuts that only I know. I know this land now and I know how to hide. I know how to disappear behind trees. I know how to disappear inside trees.

Already I feel myself to be half ghost, slinking around these woods over rotted logs with the slow-moving snakes and field mice.

I hear the men shout and talk of their plans to kill the man they have. I try and see what I can. The man is a black man.

They all stop talking and I think they have heard me, but instead a screech owl calls. They take trigger notice. Everybody knows a screech owl's call means death is somewhere near. The black man is the only one to turn and see me. Our eyes catch. The man is Sunny Rise, Jess Still's pa. And I think, *How can this be?* They killed Jess Still and now his pa, Sunny Rise?

I put my finger to my lips. Sunny Rise nods.

"It's witchy out here tonight," someone says. It's Smasher, and I can tell from the sound of his voice that he is not trying to scare. He *is* scared.

I feel something warm and furry near my foot. It is a skunk—I must not smell human to it. I must smell animal. Quietly and very very slowly, I climb the tree next to me, and the skunk waddles away. I am right above all the men. I shake down some tree ice.

"Cold ice is falling from the sky, Mark," someone says.

I hear, "Who that be?" and "It's somebody." I hear, "Who that there?" and "This here me." I hear, "Could you mind?"

I call like a screech owl.

Sunny Rise takes notice and slowly backs away from the men who have gotten down from their horses to look around. They take a few steps further and one of the men screams like a little girl. He holds up one of the old soldier leg bones, for they stand right smack in the land of the bones. They all of them scream and take off their hoods and I lean down from my tree branch to get a closer look at their faces. The moon is low and dim tonight, but when the clouds pass I see the bright red hair of Rew Smith. He has taken off his little, white costume hood and he is standing there, wailing like a little girl.

I hear Mr. Smith yelling at Rew to quit whining. "They're just bones."

"They're prob'ly just Indian bones," I hear Pappy say. He is without his hood because I have his hood.

I can see that Sunny Rise has gotten away. He has run away, but the men still have not taken notice because they are too fearful for themselves.

I see the white tail of the skunk again, coming back now with a whole family of skunks. I shake more tree ice and it falls on the skunk family. All that ice and the men yelling get the skunks good and mad, and with the smell comes more yelling, and finally the clouds pass again and I can see Pappy hitting Smasher on the top of the head with a thigh bone, shouting, "He got away," and Smasher is shouting, "*We* got to get out of here, now!" And Rew Smith is still standing there front and center, wailing wailing wailing.

I do not laugh because I cannot. I think of Sunny Rise, worried now, because he has seen the face of at least one of his murderers and they know this.

The next morning I wake up in my cave, hearing the sound of women's voices. Three Choctaw women are at the creek in front of my cave, making cane baskets by shaving oak and hickory branches and soaking them under water.

They are a mighty pretty sight in their frocks of brightly colored calico, their hair in long braids, tied up with ropes and ribbons. The clouds feather across the sky like so many chicken wings. I cut notch number thirty in my stick and recall last night, wondering if it was a dream. It is not long before the women are all singing Choctaw songs. How can this beautiful world contain such ugliness as I have seen?

People. They are like lightning sometimes. Unexpected, beautiful, and scary—mostly you can't run away from either one.

I wish I could raise enough pep to sing along with the women, but I am so tired and I have a powerful hunger.

I used to be glad it didn't matter what I wore or what I looked like because nobody but the animals saw me. But watching the women, seeing what they're wearing and how they're working together, makes me remember how it was to be in the kitchen or outside stirring a pot with Momma and other women, and remembering Momma sets me to wishing I was amongst women.

Why did my momma leave me behind? I could have kept up. I could have helped out. When I find her, I will ask her. Maybe I will be mad for a good long while, but then maybe she and I will set ourselves to working like these Choctaw women before me. We will work alongside each other again. We will stir a pot of soup or wash out some clothes and all the angry thoughts about Momma will finally leave me alone.

The Choctaw women sing what they are singing and say what they are saying and I can't understand a word of it, but it is good to hear their woman talk, their voices rising and falling, first talking all at once, then slowing. Hearing them is like listening to music.

And I can't help it. I forget myself and I start to hum to their talking. One of the women looks up.

It is Zula. She is not pregnant anymore. She carries a baby now in a sack hanging down in front of her. When she sees me she holds up her hand.

Chapter 10

Zula and the other two Choctaw women take me to their camp a ways up the river where I have not gone. We do not talk as we walk, which is fine by me. I am not their captive, though I suppose I could feel like one because I have no choice but to follow.

Their camp is nicer than my cave. They have small, neat one-room cabins like settled folk, built along the banks of the river. There are small patches of tilled land ready to be planted with corn or potatoes, and a few flocks of chickens.

When that man Mr. Tempy sees me, he throws his hands up over his little red head and shouts, "I knew you would come for a visit!"

Even though he is white, Mr. Tempy is dressed like the other Choctaw men. He is wearing moccasins and buckskin, silver armbands and wristbands. There are other white men here like Mr. Tempy.

Most of the women are wearing red skirts and calico shirts. They wear their hair parted in the middle and braided behind. When she sees me staring at the bright red part in her hair, Zula lowers her head to let me touch it as she explains that she and the other women trace a line of vermilion in their parts to represent the path of the sun.

Mr. Tempy says it is a good night for me to visit because tomorrow is a ball game. He tells me that before ball games men and women gather around sacred fires.

I am not used to all this talking. I stare at their mouths as they tell me things. I am glad they are not asking questions because I wonder what language I would speak if I spoke and if it would come out as animal or human. I hope that I can recall all that good English Mr. Frank taught me.

When the sun goes down we sit around the fires Zula says

are sacred. We eat. Each family has their one bowl. Zula and Mr. Tempy have me eat from their bowl even though I am not family. I don't have to be Choctaw to know that this means something.

We feast on wild turkey and pumpkin.

The women sit in a circle and sing. The men stand outside the circle and play their chichicouas, which are gourds filled with pebbles. Zula tells me the names of their things and their dances—the turtle dance and the tick dance.

"It is a bad time for the Choctaw," Zula says. "This bright path has led us to darkness. We have lost our homes and now we are wanderers."

The turtle dancers sing and Zula tells me what their words mean: "A life in the wilderness with plenty of meat, fish, fowl, and the turtle dance is far better than our old homes, and the corn, and the fruit, and the heart-melting fear of the dreadful Europeans."

"Who are the Europeans?" I ask.

"Anglos," Zula says.

The tick dancers trace out a sacred circle in the high grass and stomp on imaginary ticks. "The ticks are the first boatload of Anglos," Zula whispers.

"Who are the Anglos?" I ask.

"Pale." Zula looks around, trying to find the word. "Tempy. You."

"So you want to stomp us?"

Zula laughs and brings bread to her lips with her fingers. "Not all of you."

The dancing and singing go on through the night. When she sees that I am tired, Zula takes me to her cabin and makes me a pallet on the floor next to hers. She and her baby and I sleep side by side. The rest are still outside, dancing now, not singing, and through the window we can see the far-off glow of their sacred fires.

The next morning, Mr. Tempy tells me he is riding into town, into Raleigh, and he sure would like some company.

I look at Zula. I look around this fine camp and at the women fixing to go down to the water to make baskets. I thank him and say no. I'd rather stay here with Zula. I miss the company of women.

When Mr. Tempy leaves, I set out with the women while the men set out with their bows and arrows to bring down big and small game. We walk forever, it seems, walking in a straight line. Zula carries her baby in the sack hanging down in front of her. Zula tells me her ancestors named one part of the stream, the part with the white sand, Oka Bogue, which means "The Creek of Clear Water." They like the creek for the curative herbs and waters.

We settle down near the water and begin. They teach me with their hands, and all day we make baskets from the oak and hickory trees. Some of these baskets we weave tight enough to hold water. Zula's baby is a good baby and gurgles and giggles at the sound of our voices and the running water and the bobwhites calling.

I stay on like this, living among the Choctaw for as long as it is cold. I add twenty more notches to my stick of wood, making fifty days and nights that I have been away.

I learn from Zula about herbs and teas she mixes together herself. I learn from Zula about shaping a baby's head after it is born. I learn from Zula how to play chunky and other games of chance. I learn the word for mosquitoes is *marangouins.* I see the colors of Zula's baskets, colors she squeezes from the land, colors that have names I did not know before. We don't talk so much as we do. That's how I learn. I do as they do. I do as Zula does.

I get a hankering for books and I ask Zula if she has something for me to read.

"The Choctaw has no need for books," she says. "When he wishes to make known his views, like his fathers before him, he speaks from his mouth. Writing gives birth to error and feuds. When the great spirit talks, we hear him in the thunder, in the rushing winds and the mighty water."

"You want me to recite you a poem, then?" I ask.

I recite what I can remember from the poem Mr. Frank learned me. It's a poem called "Ode on a Grecian Urn," and even though I miss most of the middle, I'm real clear on the ending.

When old age shall this generation waste,
Thou shalt remain, in midst of other woe
Than ours, a friend to man, to whom thou say'st,
"Beauty is truth, truth beauty,—that is all
Ye know on earth, and all ye need to know."

"You are so young to know such wisdom," she says. "Much time has passed since I have heard such words."

"Oh, I didn't write that. I just recited it."

"But you are wise enough to remember. You are wise to know."

"I need more than a poem," I say.

* * *

One night before we both fall to sleep, Zula whispers to me, "The Anglos are looking for you." We sleep side by side just like every other night in our own women's cabin. Mr. Tempy has just come back from being gone, and he has spoken to Zula. "They have Mr. Frank in jail and Miss Irene is expecting a baby. They are saying that Mr. Frank has something to do with that black man Sunny Rise."

"Who's they?"

"A Mr. Smith. And your father."

"What happened to Sunny Rise?"

"He ran away and nobody can find him. They say Mr. Frank kidnapped him and walked him to a boat that took him north. They say he does such things."

I think on this. It could be true. He and his pa walked Buck to freedom. "But why would that land Mr. Frank in jail?"

"Sunny Rise owes money to a Mr. Smith. Now Mr. Smith says Mr. Frank has to pay him. This Mr. Smith demands an arrest warrant for Mr. Frank."

"I thought there was an arrest warrant for Mr. Smith and my pappy."

"They caught them, then set them free. Law says there were no eyewitnesses. No evidence."

"That's crazy," I say, knowing I am the *eye* in *eyewitness*.

"Anglos," Zula says. "They are full up with too much noise."

We both think and we don't say anything. We can hear the low talk of men's voices outside around the fires.

"Court's in session, and I want Frank to know that I'm on his side," Mr. Tempy tells me the next morning. "I'll be honest with you, Addy. Our friend needs your help."

"But what can I do?"

"Addy, Irene told me you know some things about that fire at the schoolhouse. Just tell people what you know."

"Is Mr. Frank asking for me? Did he say he needed me?"

"He doesn't know what he needs," Mr. Tempy says. "Besides, Frank never asks for help. You and I both know that."

I feel my legs and arms shaking like they're cold. I feel my chin quiver and my eyes tear up. This comes over me all at once and I don't know why. "I'd have to tell on my pappy," I whisper. "I'm not strong like you or Mr. Frank. I don't think I can cross family."

Mr. Tempy puts his arm around me and my shaking settles some. "I'm not going to tell you it's easy, because it's not. I left my family up north. Hardest thing I ever did. But I found my own family here. You'll be fine. You're stronger than you know."

Zula takes me by the hand.

"Where are you taking her?" Mr. Tempy says.

"The Choctaw always thinks," she says. "We need time to answer."

"But she's not even Choctaw!"

Zula doesn't bother answering Mr. Tempy. She leads me to a cabin off in the distance, set apart from the others. She tells me she will perform rites to secure divine favor and ensure that my passage into the outside world will be successful.

"But I haven't said I'm going to Raleigh," I say. "Not yet."

"Words," Zula says. "Too many words."

She paints me white as though I am not white, as though I am Choctaw. Up close, Zula smells of sage. She says that I am crossing boundaries and that I must prepare myself for the transformation from order to disorder. She says I must respect these boundaries to maintain order in my world. We drink tea she has brewed special. It is minty and musty-tasting and it makes me open my eyes wide.

Together we sit alone in this hut made for crossings.

I tell Zula about the little man in my dreams. I tell her that after sleeping amongst the Choctaw, I think that he has left me for good. I tell Zula about my dreams and she tells me the little man's name because she says she knows all about him.

"That is Kwanokasha," she says. "He is one of the border

guards. He lives in caves in the rough and broken part of the country, searching for young children whom he captures and brings to his cave where three spirits live. The child who takes the knife will grow up to be a murderer. The one who fancies the poisonous herbs will never be able to help others. But you took the medicinal herbs," she says, looking me over, taking my hand. "You will be a healer."

I laugh. "Me? Don't you know the O'Donnells? I think I was born to be one of those others. Not a healer."

Zula is not laughing. She is shaking her head. "I do not know this tribe O'Donnell. I only know Anglo and Addy. You have met up with Kwanokasha. He has wanted to influence you during your crossing. But you? You have chosen good medicine. You mean to help people."

"No," I say. "I'm just mean. I'm an O'Donnell and that's what everyone says about us."

Zula, she just smiles.

"I knew I recognized you. I knew the first time I saw you across the river, when you were with your friend. You and I. We are both healers."

Mr. Tempy and I ride together on one horse all morning, and when we get to Raleigh, we see children playing in the street.

The children look so young and small and they make so much noise, more noise than I've heard children make in a long, long time. They look up at me, riding with Mr. Tempy. They point and stare. They say, "Here come Injuns." They say, "Look at that little boy Injun riding with his pappy."

I am glad now for Zula's paint. I am glad for the disguise.

Mr. Tempy whispers to me about Raleigh. Court officials and jurors stay at the hotel owned by Mr. Childre across the street from the courthouse. They talk politics and court cases. They are there now, sitting on the big front porch, dressed in their Sunday best.

He tells me that the main room of the hotel has bullet holes in the ceiling from when Mr. Childre was mistaken for a deserter from the Confederate army and shot at. As we pass the hotel, we hear the tinny piano and plinking banjos from inside. The doors open wide then and all of Mr. Childre's children come running out. He shouts out to them to scat. He says he does not want his children or his wife mixed up in the dirty affairs of the country. He says this loud enough for everyone to hear, then he eyeballs Mr. Tempy and me as we ride past.

Mr. Tempy tethers his horse. I am shaking all over again and I think that my knees will give out from under me. Mr.

Tempy, he takes my hand and puts what looks like a tooth on my palm.

"That there's a bear claw. It's what I took from Kwanokasha. It's helped me some. Maybe you can get something out of it too."

I put the bear claw in my pocket and walk into the courthouse with Mr. Tempy. People stop talking and stare. I hear, "Who let in the Injuns?" I hear, "They're not Injuns, just dressed like Injuns." Mr. Tempy heads for the front, but I pull his sleeve and we sit down close to the back.

Rew Smith is sitting there in front of us next to his pappy, Mr. Smith. He looks at me, then pinches his nose with his fingers.

"He smells like dirt," he says of me. His pappy laughs.

I am glad Rew does not recognize me. I sniff myself and it's true I whiff of dried leaves, mud, and acorns, but what of it? Leastways I don't eat dirt. My cousins in No-Bob eat dirt, but not me.

I have been gone and away in the woods for a good long time. I have been quiet with myself and listened only to screech owls and squirrels, deer and turkeys, Zula and other women in the tribe. Here in this town of Raleigh, Mississippi, there is only noise noise noise. Zula is right. Us Anglos are full up with too much noise and too many words. My ears ring with all the words. Children running around, screaming in the streets, women inside whispering whispering, and the men brawling in the Harrison Hotel, singing, shouting, and making more noise. They can't sit quiet. They can't sit still. When do they think? *Do* they think?

When Pappy comes into the courthouse, I can hardly stand to look at him. He needs cleaning up some, with his craggy eyebrows and big ears. He looks like one more dirty O'Donnell child. I have not been there to care for him.

Pappy passes me without recognizing me. I am invisible to him.

Then I hear the talk start up. I hear a lady whisper to another lady, "Those O'Donnells? Meanest folks what ever lived." The other lady whispers back, "It's them kind of folks what's got things so tore up now." I hear, "I've never known an O'Donnell to come off the loser." I hear, "They just like a little fun and mischief. They're not *bad*." I hear someone say Mark O'Donnell, my pappy, has killed as many as fifty men in his lifetime. The number is there without the funny stories.

Pappy takes his seat right in front of me and Mr. Tempy. He sits next to Mr. Smith and Rew. He is right in front of me, so close I can smell the oil he put in his dirty hair to smooth it back. I can smell his whiskey breath as he whispers something to Mr. Smith. I can see his frayed collar, the comb tracks on the back of his head, the caked dirt on the back of his neck and behind his ears. I want to shake him and scream, *Pappy, why did you ever leave Momma and me?*

Then the sheriff brings in Mr. Frank. Oh, but he looks tired and pale. I catch a glimpse of Miss Irene up front, big with child. When they look at each other, they both look glad to see each other and not. I understand this. They want to see each other, miss each other, but not here, not this way. Mr. Frank is shamed. He sits at a table with his lawyer, without his wife, without his family.

Miss Irene sits directly behind Mr. Frank.

The judge comes in, we stand up, and he thumps his big gavel on his desk, calling for all of us to settle down and listen up. Two men stand in front of his desk, whispering their whispers. These men in suits are lawyers.

One of the lawyers takes his seat with Mr. Frank. The other signals to Mr. Smith, who says to everyone around him, "This shouldn't take too long." Pappy and Rew laugh and straighten themselves, proud to know the man who steps up to the front of the courtroom to sit with his very own lawyer.

As the sheriff walks toward the back of the courtroom, Mr. Tempy gets his attention. The sheriff comes over and Mr.

Tempy whispers something to him, pointing toward me. The sheriff hurries to the front of the courtroom and whispers to Mr. Frank's lawyer.

It seems they're all through with accusing Mr. Frank of taking Sunny Rise out of town and out of state. We learn too that someone has taken a good bit of courtroom time proving that Sunny Rise owed Mr. Smith a thousand dollars, and because Mr. Frank took Sunny Rise away, it is up to Mr. Frank to pay up.

They are into the let's-hear-what-you-have-to-say-for-yourself part.

Mr. Smith's lawyer calls Little Bit to the stand. She is wearing a fine new peach-colored calico dress. The lawyer asks her questions about what all her brother Mr. Frank has been doing. I pray that Little Bit keeps her head.

"Is your brother a member of any organization that you know of?"

Little Bit thinks on this. "The church."

Folks laugh.

"How about the Ku Klux Klan?"

"No, sir! Not my brother. He says it's nothing but evil."

Many folks whisper and I can't hear what they are saying.

The lawyer smiles at all of us in the courtroom, smiling like not being a member of the Klan is something bad.

"See, my brother helped rebuild that schoolhouse that the men with the hoods burned down to the ground. The sheriff is still looking for the men who did that, and me and Addy O'Donnell saw it all. That night."

Everybody in the room, they all start to talk at once.

The lawyer keeps on smiling, like he thinks this little girl is real funny. "Miss Russell."

"Little Bit," Little Bit says.

"Little Bit. It would be impossible to identify any of the men from that night because they were all wearing hoods. You said so yourself."

"But I know their shoes," she says, just as sure as she can be. Mr. Smith and Pappy just snicker.

"Show me a shoe and I'll show you the man," Little Bit says. She tells the judge and the jury what kind and what color shoes two of the men wore. "I'm closer to the ground than most people," Little Bit tells the judge.

The judge nods and says just to make sure that Mr. Frank is not a Klan member and was not there that night of the fire, breaking the law, he'd like to see Mr. Frank's shoes. When Mr.

Frank stands, we all see that he is wearing shoes he has made himself on his land and these are not the shoes that Little Bit described.

Mr. Smith and Pappy are not laughing anymore. Pappy tucks in his legs so that his feet are under his seat.

The lawyer says, "Frank Russell is your brother, is he not, young lady?"

"Yes, sir, he is, sir."

"And you would do anything for him, would you not?"

"Yes, sir."

"Including lie?"

She thinks about this. "No, sir. Ma and Pa taught me not to lie. So did Frank."

A few of the folks laugh. When Little Bit is excused, she walks straight to the back of the courthouse toward me and Mr. Tempy.

"See?" she whispers to me. "I told you I'm not some Little Miss Priss."

She is the only one to recognize me. Only she would.

We both of us smile at each other. She was sitting up front with her ma and pa, Mr. Frank's parents. Jack is there too, taken to sucking his thumb again. I wish Little Bit could sit by me.

Then she takes a seat right by me. She squirms to fit. She's giggly and sweet-smelling and having too much fun. She takes my hand, then with her other wipes away some of Zula's white paint from around my eyes. She laughs and whispers, "Sure good to see you again, Addy O'Donnell."

She presses something into the palm of my hand. Paper. It is the folded-up map we buried inside the jar under Mr. Frank's praying log.

Mr. Frank's lawyer calls Mr. Frank to have a seat and to tell him about his most recent trip to New Orleans. Turns out that since Mr. Frank had all his goods stolen on his first trip, he went again. That's when Sunny Rise disappeared, that night I saw the men in the land of the bones. While Mr. Frank was gone.

Mr. Frank talks about his purchases in New Orleans and how the next morning, when he was ready to leave town, he went down to the French Market and had a breakfast of fish, oysters, and coffee.

"How are we to believe that you were in New Orleans and not with Sunny Rise?" Mr. Frank's lawyer asks, and I can't help but wonder whose side he's on.

"Well, I did meet up with an acquaintance in New Orleans. Garner O'Donnell."

People all around us start to whisper.

"When did you see Garner?"

"The night I was in New Orleans. The night Sunny disappeared. Garner and I took dinner together."

"That all?"

Mr. Frank looks at Miss Irene and lowers his head. He clears his throat and says softly, "We had a drink together. At a saloon."

Some of the women in the courthouse draw their breath in. Some of the men in the courthouse laugh out loud. Miss Irene just stares quietly on.

Mr. Frank steps down, and the lawyer calls Garner O'Donnell to the stand. Garner swears in and takes the stand. He testifies that he had dinner and a drink with Mr. Frank in New Orleans the night Sunny Rise disappeared.

Mr. Frank's lawyer says that's all he wants to ask Garner, but then Mr. Smith's lawyer steps up and asks Garner, "Mr. O'Donnell, weren't you in this very court before? Weren't you the very man who once tried to cheat Frank Russell out of his own land?"

"I wasn't cheating . . ."

"Answer the question," the judge says.

"Yes, sir. I am the same man."

"And now you say you had a friendly drink with Frank Russell in New Orleans?"

"Yes, sir."

"And you expect us to believe you?"

"Yes, sir."

"What did the two of you discuss?"

Garner clears his throat. "Business, mostly," he says. "And my niece Addy. Frank took in Addy when her momma left her. I thanked Frank for that. I bought him a drink."

People in the courtroom mumble, but I can't hear what they're saying.

When Garner steps down, he passes Mr. Frank and nods. Mr. Frank does not nod back. He has his head down like he can't even look at Garner even though Garner has done him a kind of favor.

I see Mr. Frank lean back to whisper something to Miss Irene. I guess that he's hoping he has not brought her shame. I see her hold his hand and smile. I hear her say, "I love you, Frank Russell."

This is the love that is good in a marriage. This is the love that Momma and Pappy never had. This here in front of me is a proud love, a quiet, honorable love. This love rises above fierce love and smashing lips.

I envy the both of them. I envy Garner too because he has finished his own hard work.

When I hear my name called I think that I will faint before I stand up. It is my turn. It is my turn and I am not sure at all what I am there for, what this lawyer will ask me, and if I can remember the words to use to talk.

Everybody is talking at once. Mr. Smith's lawyer says, "Addy O'Donnell is not in the courtroom. In fact, Addy O'Donnell has long disappeared. She's probably somewhere with Sunny Rise." The people in the courtroom laugh, all except Pappy.

Little Bit squeezes my hand. "Just tell the truth," she whispers. Truth should be easier than it is. I recall that poem by Mr. John Keats. The one I told Zula. Truth is beauty and beauty is truth and that's all you need to know. That is powerful troublesome. For I have seen some of the ugliest truth and it was not beautiful.

I stand up. People all around me look at me and whisper as I stand. Pappy. He doesn't even turn around. And I cannot look at him.

I put my hand on the Bible. I swear to tell the truth. Then, I take my stand.

Mr. Frank's lawyer asks me easy questions first. My name. Where I've been. Then I tell things in order. I tell the story of the night Little Bit and I took a walk in the woods and saw all the men at the schoolhouse while the Negroes sang church songs. I tell how I saw one of the men light the cross and how he looked up at the burning. I describe the hood he wore. I tell how I tried to save that little boy, Jess Still. "These are not stories I embroider," I say. "These here are facts."

Then I tell of what I saw in the woods, how I watched these men get ready to kill Sunny Rise. I tell of how all the costumed men got spooked in the land of the bones, how I shook down ice, and how a family of skunks scattered them all away.

"How are we to believe what you are telling us when you were the only witness?" the lawyer says. Again, I'm thinking, *Whose side are you on?*

But it is a good question. I am an O'Donnell. I'm not sure I would believe me either.

I hold up the folded piece of paper and unfold for him the map of that first night, the night the schoolhouse burned down. He looks at it.

"Objection, Your Honor," Mr. Smith's lawyer says. "Anybody could have drawn that any time." But I can hear the scare in his voice.

"It's dated," I say, pointing out the date Little Bit wrote in the corner.

"That doesn't refute my point, Your Honor," Mr. Smith's lawyer says.

"I'm not lying," I say. It's the best I can do.

The judge wants to see. The jury wants to see. There is a good deal of grumbling and talk. Then the judge turns to me and says, "Addy? Do you have any other evidence you can provide from that night or from the night that Mr. Sunny Rise disappeared?"

I think and think and think until my head itches.

"Ask Mrs. Smith and the other wives how their husbands smelled that night, the night Sunny Rise disappeared," I say.

And all at once, all female voices in the courthouse let out a moan. Some laughed, but I could hear others say how they spent weeks soaking this or that in tomatoes to get the smell of skunk out.

And their men? They like to froze.

These wives were crossing with their husbands' business without even knowing.

"Anything else you witness, Addy?" the judge asks.

I don't know what comes over me. Maybe O'Donnell mischief. I say, "I watched Rew Smith cry like a baby."

"I wasn't scared at all," Rew screams, standing up all of a

sudden. "I did everything my daddy told me to do." His pappy, Mr. Smith, shushes him, tells him to sit back down. Pappy, he slaps the back of Rew's legs until Rew whimpers and sits.

"Anything else?" the judge asks me.

Out from my pocket I pull the smelly, dirty, balled-up hood and I hold it up for all to see, making sure they see how it's the hood that matches the hood in the drawing. Same one with the fancy slits all around.

"Where did you get that, Addy?" the judge asks.

"It's my pappy's. I took it off him when he was sleeping, the morning I left him."

Everyone turns to look at Pappy.

Mr. Frank's lawyer clears his throat and addresses the jury. "Gentlemen, we have here a set of men who have established for themselves their own law. They put their foot upon the criminal code and trampled it in the dust. They may and they do commit murder. But we do protest and shall with our dying breath protest against an aristocracy of crime. This man? Frank Russell? He is guilty of nothing more than being a fine, upstanding citizen of Smith County."

The judge says that due to the circumstances, Frank

Russell is clear of all charges. Then he calls Mr. Smith and Mark O'Donnell to the stand. Pappy takes a long time to saunter up to the judge's desk.

"Those are the shoes!" Little Bit says as loud as I ever heard her. "Those are the shoes I told you I seen that night." And everyone in the room is talking at once as we all look at the very shoes Little Bit described in her own testimony.

The judge hammers his gavel down on his desk over and over and tells everyone to settle down. I am still sitting there in the witness stand when the judge charges both Mr. Smith and Pappy with murder and setting fire to government property, "among other misdeeds," he adds. Then he asks them if there's anything they want to say for themselves.

Mr. Smith shakes his head.

"I come home to clean up No-Bob," Pappy starts, turning around toward the jury and the courtroom, running his hands through his hair. That's what he does when he is nervous. I can hear the nerves in his voice too. He is trying to sound courtroom-like.

A few women whisper. Most all of us wait for more.

He looks past all of us and up at the rafters of the building. He stands there, staring. If I had his fiddle, I would hand it to him now. It's as though he is standing in front of a beautiful woman and he is no longer sure if he has the courage to ask her to dance. He tilts back and forth, seems to think better of it, then looks past everyone and straight at me.

"I'll meet you in heaven, Addy O'Donnell," he says to me. People who said this to Pappy before said it like a threat. But when he says this to me, he says it sweet, like a nice promise, and I don't know what to think or say.

Now I think I know what that John Keats fellow means about truth. Once the truth is all laid out in front of you and everybody else and the whole world to see, truth good and bad, it *is* a sight to behold, and that sight might be where beauty lies sleeping.

"I still love you, Pappy," I whisper.

The judge thumps down his gavel and says we're finished for the day. The sheriff handcuffs first Mr. Smith, then Pappy, and takes them both to the hotel because they have not yet built a prison for white people.

That night the courthouse catches fire and burns down to the ground. Some say Pappy did it. Some say he had his friends and family do it for him. All the records from the day's court session and the year's before this day burn up along with the building.

But he knows. Pappy knows. And I know. We don't need anything writ down to know about the truth.

The prison room at the hotel is wide open and empty, and nobody can find either Mr. Smith or Pappy.

Pappy said I could never run away from family, but I did. I did because I had to. Now he's the one running. Running away from both the law and himself. I figure out now that it's a fact that Pappy never did go to Texas. He just camped out in the swamps all that time he was away from Momma and me.

Maybe this time he has run off to Texas for real.

Chapter 11

It is spring. The dogwoods are in bloom and the whole world is popping. Already, Miss Irene planted verbena, old maids, phlox, and four-o'clocks around the house, just to set it off right, and Mr. Frank has planted his fields. I plant the kitchen garden with every seed I can lay my hands on. Four kinds of beans, peas, lettuce, okra, peppers, squash, turnips. I plant watermelons and mush melons in the loamy dirt near the creek. I plant and plant and plant, for they have taken me back in. Miss Irene and Mr. Frank have taken me back into their home.

We got ourselves a new preacher. This new preacher says sin is the cause of the world being in the fix it's in today. The only way to fight sin is to get together, and getting together is all right by me.

We all go for Easter service at the new church built on Clear Creek. On the way, we pass a new horsepower cotton gin, made from steel from Mobile. I ride with Mr. Frank's parents, Little Bit, and Jack. Mr. Frank and Miss Irene ride together. Miss Irene is about ready to burst with child.

The preacher tells us about the legend of the dogwood. At the time of the crucifixion of Jesus, the dogwood attained the size of the oak and other forest trees, and because it was so strong and firm, the wood was chosen as the timber for the cross. To be thus used for such a cruel purpose greatly distressed the tree. Jesus, as he hung nailed upon it, sensed the tree's distress and, in his gentle pity for all sorrow, said to the tree, "Because of your regret and pity for my suffering I make you a promise that never again shall the dogwood tree grow large enough to be used for a cross. Henceforth, it shall be slender and bent and twisted, and its blossoms shall be in the form of a cross, two long petals and two short petals, and in the center of the outer edge of each petal there will be nail prints brown with rust and stained with blood, and in the center of the flower will be a crown of thorns, that all who see it may remember it was upon a dogwood tree that the Lord was crucified, and this tree shall not be mutilated nor destroyed, but cherished and protected as a reminder of my agony and death upon the cross."

After the preaching, Mrs. Davenport makes announcements about the boxed suppers. Every woman should put together a boxed supper to be auctioned at the church to raise money for a new piano.

Little Bit, Jack, and me, we all say, "Aaahh," just thinking on the sound of a piano.

"Well, I'll be," Miss Irene says after the service ends. She holds her stomach as Mr. Frank helps her into their new buggy. "I never knew any of that about dogwood."

"Jesus sure was something," Little Bit says, climbing in with me. We sit in the back and let our legs hang off the edge.

Mr. Frank laughs, taking hold of his mule's reins. "Yes, he was. He opened his heart to the presence of love."

"If I do that, could I hear a tree talk?" Little Bit wants to know.

* * *

We all go back to Mr. Frank's, where there are potatoes on the coals and bacon in the iron pan. There is bread, molasses, meat, sweet potatoes, pot likker, milk, fried chicken, boiled ham, banana cake, and homemade pickles. I set to work and help serve everyone who can find a chair. Then I sit down too with a loaded plate, and as I eat, my eyes water when I think that the one cure for this hollow feeling is eating until your hollow stomach is full up with good things.

A friend of Mr. Frank's pa has come after the service to join us too. He tells how he fought in four battles during the war, then he was captured and put in prison on Ship Island, where he was held and guarded by Negroes for thirty-eight days. He was never wounded, but in Rome, Georgia, his belt was shot from around him and his clothes were set on fire by the bullet. In Vicksburg, they set him free and he walked home, swimming the Pearl River. He never learned to read, so he was glad to hear that story that the preacher told about the dogwood.

He and Mr. Frank's pa talk of an old war veterans' gathering in Oktibbeha County, a reunion to commemorate the Confederacy. I suppose if I had been through something as big as a war, I would want to see the others who had too, but I'm tired of hearing about the war and all that fighting.

Mr. Frank's ma, she says, "Haven't we all had enough

fighting and destruction to last a lifetime? I for one don't need to sit around and remember it."

Mr. Frank laughs and says how once upon a time, he imagined Yankee soldiers as cruel monsters blowing fire and smoke.

"And then you saw one up close," his pa says.

They both nod and they are quiet.

I think on this. I think how you think about people in lumps, and then you get to know one and all that thinking changes. I think of how Mr. Frank's pa lived in a world of slavery, how he might have looked at someone like Sunny Rise and thought *slave,* and how now he might look at him and think *man.* I think about how Mr. Frank sees me as Addy and not an O'Donnell termite. I think about how I saw the Choctaw as a people who had no real home. Then I met Zula.

Miss Irene brings out a coconut cake and Mr. Frank's ma opens up a jar of her fine peaches.

Everybody is talking at once and eating at once.

Mr. Frank is talking about supplementing what he earns with the store he's got up and running and his teacher's income of ten dollars a term. He's saying that with the railroad and the easier traveling, and now that it's safer—that's when he winks at me—he could start a peddling wagon to go along with his store.

Mr. Frank's pappy listens, then he stops and looks at me. My mouth is full so I keep chewing. "Frank? This girl, Addy." Mr. Frank's pappy doesn't say anything for a minute and I think by the serious sound of his voice that he will finally throw me out, just because I am an O'Donnell and he can't stand to think about O'Donnells after what they done to his son. I swallow. "Addy. She saved you same as you saved me once. You know that?"

Mr. Frank, he smiles.

"That's right, Pa."

"Happy Easter, Addy," Mr. Frank's pappy says to me, raising his coffee cup.

He sits at the head of the table and doesn't eat any of the sweets, though before him is a spread so fine, I can hardly keep my mouth shut. I am so happy I melt down.

Mr. Frank's pa looks to have everything but food on his mind. He recollects a heap about slavery times and we all listen and eat. He talks about the long ago. He tells us how he and his soldier pal would march behind a wagon, and when the wagon wheel smashed over a frog, he and his friend would pick it up, shake the dust off it, and eat it. Some of us laugh but Mr. Frank's pappy doesn't. They were that hungry, he says. He says isn't it fine how his son can provide for us all with so much bounty. Then he lays his knife down like he is real tired, and he stops talking.

"What's wrong with Mr. Frank's pa?" I say.

Then Mr. Frank gets up and leans over his pa and says, "Pa? Pa?"

"Jack? Jack?" Mr. Frank's ma asks.

And Lord help that poor man, for he is dead. Mr. Frank's pa is dead.

When Mr. Frank sees my uncle Garner O'Donnell coming down the road, and when Garner tells him his intentions, Mr. Frank just stares. As an act of kindness and sympathy for Mr. Frank, Garner says he has come over to help Frank dress and put his pa away. He will help Mr. Frank bury his pa. Garner rolls up his sleeves, then shows Mr. Frank that he has brought over a razor to use to shave Mr. Frank's pa before Mr. Frank dresses then buries him.

Mr. Frank leans on the door frame, looking down at his shoes. The two of them don't say anything as Mr. Frank looks to be trying to decide. I figure he will shut the door. But he lets him in. Mr. Frank lets him in, and I can see by the way Garner puts his hand on Mr. Frank's shoulder that these two here are not just friends who drink together, not like Smasher and

Pappy or Mr. Smith and Pappy. These two men have come to an understanding betwixt themselves. Once upon a time they argued, even fought over some land, and now, now they are friends. They are friends.

They are in the house together for quite some time.

Miss Irene cooks some chicken and Mr. Frank's ma makes bread. I sweep. As we work together in the kitchen, and as Garner works in the parlor room, we are quiet like the woods are quiet.

Later we get word from Garner that the law caught up with my pappy and tried him in Jackson, and they put him in jail.

I think how Pappy swore he would never spend time in jail because it would kill him to be behind bars.

What with Mr. Frank's pa dead, I see all the love and kindness that the Russells show their kin. And all the mourning makes me sorrowful sad for all the love that I missed from my own kin.

Even in the middle of all this sadness, I get to hating Pappy, and it isn't easy hating Pappy. People say he was the meanest devil that ever lived on the Lord's green earth. Others say he was the funniest. Which is it? Either-or? Or is it both?

He is like a monster that way, and over and over I hate hate

hate. But once I just plain think of him as Pappy, once I see him plain, as a man, pitiful and scared as he was standing in front of the judge at the courthouse in Raleigh, caught, I feel sorry for him, and when I feel sorry for him, the hating goes away and everything flattens out and I can sleep again.

Mr. Frank's pa had told his wife he wanted to be buried under the peach tree north of the house, and this is what they do.

They have a quiet ceremony. I think of what Zula would do. I think about the comfort of her actions. I think about how maybe Zula and Mr. Frank's pa would have liked each other. He was always calm-like and saving his words.

I think of what people leave behind when they die. At school, Mr. Frank told us that when George Washington died, he owned fifty-seven mules. He was called the father of mule-breeding and now mules are more important than oxen in farm work.

I think of all that dies with Mr. Russell—all his recollections, all his memories and love. So much in one body.

I do what the Choctaw do when they mourn. It helps Little Bit to help. We make a fire outside the Russells' house and keep it lit to appease the spirit of the dead and to keep it warm.

We all, each of us, have our ways of saying goodbye to the dead and comforting those who themselves have to say goodbye.

At Mr. Frank's boyhood home, Little Bit and me sit under a tree she says used to be called the freak tree. She says it got hit by lightning once upon a time and got shaped like a *Y*. But the tree next to it grew and leaned into it, and together, they are now shaped like an *H*. She calls them the kissing trees.

I don't have words for the feelings I am feeling. I don't have words for such things. Her pa is dead and I'm powerful sorry for Little Bit.

I scoot closer and hope that'll do.

We read his headstone.

1820–1876

WAS ALMOST ONE MONTH WALKING TO GET BACK HOME.

LAID TO REST UNDER A BEAUTIFUL TREE HE PLANTED.

FENCED IN WITH AN IRON FENCE.

What would my headstone say?

ADDY WAS AN O'DONNELL.

HER PAPPY LEFT HER, THEN HER MOMMA LEFT HER.

WHEN HER PAPPY CAME HOME, ADDY TURNED HIM IN.

AND ADDY WAS AN O'DONNELL NO MORE.

Way out in the distance we can hear them working on the Gulf and Ship Island Railroad that will cut through our county and tie us up with the rest of the nation.

Already folks are out plowing and tilling the fields. They are planting corn, cotton, peas, and beans. They wear straw hats to keep the sun off their heads and shoulders. The men tie ropes around their necks and backs to attach themselves to the mules.

They work hard out there in those fields. There is no shade.

Little Bit and I put our heads to the trunk of the tree. We lean our ears into the bark. We press hard and listen.

Chapter 12

Little Jack comes running, shouting, yelling, for me.

"Addy, Addy," he's calling. "Come quick. Frank and Ma need you."

I don't even stop to ask, *What for?* I cannot run fast enough to help. Little Bit runs close behind me, shouting, "Wait, wait," and even though she is older than I am, she cannot run fast enough to catch up.

When we get to Mr. Frank's house, he hails us from the porch, holding Little Bit and Jack back, telling them to stay on the porch with him.

"The baby's coming, Addy. Ma's in there with Irene, but she's going to need your help. Little Bit, Jack, you stay with me. I could use your company."

He called her just "Irene." He said Miss Irene's name like she was my friend. He said they need my help.

Miss Irene, Mr. Frank's ma, and me, we stay together in that one room for twelve hours, boiling water, making tea, sitting up, and sitting down.

So many women in these parts die giving birth to a baby. Some just die from too many babies. So having this baby isn't all laughing and celebrating. It is better to be more careful than not.

Babies aren't just born—they got to fight their way into life. Seems like with all that fighting and terrible, painful bloodiness, a life would come out mean and hateful, but babies don't come like that. Not at first, anyway. They just come out hopeful, sweet, and needing.

Miss Irene is slight and weak, but when the time comes, she fights right along with that baby, and soon enough, she and Mr. Frank have themselves a baby girl.

Mr. Frank comes in from the porch looking pale and worried, his chin rattling and quivering. Then, when his ma puts that bundled-up baby in his arms, he cries. Mr. Frank, big, strong teacher, farmer-man Mr. Frank, cries like a baby, and I can't help but cry too. We are crying happy, sad, mournful tears all at once. We are crying for our passed-away pappies and our lost mommas and for the new ma and pa in this room. What a feeling this is! It is like no other choked-up, throaty feeling. It helps when I look outside the window and see a cardinal chirping on a branch. I have to open the door and swallow to clear my throat.

First thing a child ever takes in her hand will be the thing that she desires and obtains most in future life. That's why mommas and pappies in these parts press a coin into a baby's hand. But this little girl? Before she is bigger than a minute, she takes hold of her pappy's thumb.

I watch as Mr. Frank gently puts her into her crib. His ma takes out a Bible and sits down with it at the kitchen table. She shows me the page with all the recorded births of Mr. Frank, Little Bit, and then Jack.

"What are you calling her?" I ask.

"If she was a he I thought of Jack," Mr. Frank says. His ma looks up from the page. There are tears in her eyes. "After Pa."

"Hey," little Jack says. "That's my name."

"That's right. It would have been confusing. Even if

we called him Little Jack, Junior." Little Bit and Jack laugh, huddled next to the baby's crib. "Or little Little Jack," little Jack says.

Irene calls from the bed. "What about Thelma? After your mother."

Mr. Frank and his ma look at each other. "Thelma," Mr. Frank says, nodding, looking at their baby.

His ma smiles and sets to writing. "Thelma," Mr. Frank says again, looking at me, then at his baby girl. "Thelma Addy Russell."

The names take my breath away.

Looking at this baby, Thelma Addy Russell, I can't help but wonder if the world is going to be good enough for such a sweet little thing. And how can those soft, furry shoulders take on all that they will surely have to take on?

The world is a powerful place, but then again, so are we.

Some folks say that being around death and mourning make Miss Irene and her newborn baby sickly. For whatever reasons, not but a day later, Miss Irene is poorly. I feel of her pulse. She has the fever.

Little baby Thelma gets a bad case of hives and then thrush. Then she has the fever too.

Mr. Frank goes to find a doctor. His ma sets out to air and clean the house while Little Bit minds little Jack. They tend to their chores and collect pecans falling early from the trees out front.

Miss Irene, she taught me how to weave and spin. She took me in and saved my life. Least I can do is return the favor.

I go down to Clear Creek to collect what I know will help.

I know some about babies. I know the rules Momma taught me in No-Bob whenever she helped with an O'Donnell birthing. A baby must never be allowed to look into a mirror until it is a year old, for to do so would cause it to have a hard time in cutting teeth. And for a baby having a hard time teething? Put a string of coppers around its neck and he won't have no trouble at all. They teethe worse in hot weather too. When the babies have the colic, tie soot up in a rag and boil it, then give them the water. To ease the prickly heat, use rotten wood powdered up fine.

I wish Momma was here now to reshow me things and reremind me so that I can be more sure.

But Zula showed me the power of herbs. I saw for myself how one tea made from Jerusalem brushweed can get rid of worms and how another tea made from horsemint, goldenrod, and holly can bring a person back to life.

I use my pocketknife to cut the herbs. I bundle up the herbs I find and pick into my apron and then run all the way back to the house where I crush them.

For Miss Irene, I make a strong tea out of gum bark Momma used to make for herself when she got pains in her stomach. I have Miss Irene drink cup after cup while I sweep the yard with a brush broom. When I come inside and her pains are better, I use wild horehound for the chills and fever and make her a batch of life-everlasting tea.

Miss Irene sleeps for the first time without the fever.

But baby Thelma's thrush is not gone and she is still warm to the touch.

I mix together sage and catnip and brew it into a warm tea the way I seen Zula do once with a Choctaw baby who had the thrush. I use a soft boll of cotton, dip it into the tea, and swab little Thelma Addy's tongue and all inside her mouth.

Then I remember something Momma told me once. It is claimed by many in No-Bob that a person who never saw her father can cure thrush on a baby by blowing her breath in its mouth. A woman in Mize is noted for these powers, her father having been killed in the war before her birth. Babies were brought from far and near so that this woman named Elva could exert her powers. But Elva died not but a year ago.

The way I figure, I never really did see my pappy. Not nearly clear enough.

I breathe into little Thelma Addy's mouth. She yawns. I breathe into her mouth again. She breathes back at me a warm, milky breath. I feel as though others are here in the room with us. I look around but only see Miss Irene's curtains blowing from the open window. The air smells of sage. Thelma Addy's arms are as soft as Momma's hands were once.

"Momma?" I whisper. "Zula?"

I breathe into Thelma Addy's mouth again and again, feeling the presence of Momma and Zula both, and after a while, I can't help but wonder who's curing who.

"Addy? What are you doing?" Mr. Frank comes in with a doctor, a new man with long hair and whiskers named Dr. Hill.

Mr. Frank picks up little Thelma Addy. The doctor is already looking after Miss Irene.

"Your wife has no fever, Mr. Russell," Dr. Hill says.

Miss Irene opens her eyes at the new voice. "It was Addy, Frank. Addy took care of me and the baby."

Dr. Hill nods, then takes the baby from Mr. Frank. He unbundles Thelma Addy, making her cry and howl, and we all see inside her mouth now wide open—clear and pink.

"No fever," Dr. Hill says, bundling her back up and giving her to her momma. "If this baby had thrush, she doesn't have it anymore."

As payment, the doctor stays for lunch, which Mr. Frank's ma has made and brought over.

"You sure do know a lot about caring for folks," Mr. Frank says.

The doctor says yes, he does, and continues to eat. Mr. Frank laughs and says, "Well, Doc, I was talking to Addy."

I look up from my fried chicken and finish chewing, then swallow.

"Yes," Dr. Hill says, asking for more peaches and peas. "She must have had past experiences with such matters. Was your father a doctor?" This doctor sure is busy with his eating, for he hardly looks up.

"My momma used to have seasons of sickness," I say.

"Did you try cod-liver oil?" Dr. Hill asks, stopping for a minute to swallow.

"No, sir," I say.

"Well, I don't know what Miss Irene or I would do without you, Addy," Mr. Frank says.

I am sitting across from Mr. Frank at the same table and I look at him square.

"You and me both know that I've brought a good deal of trouble and heartache," I say.

Mr. Frank laughs. "You used to remind me so much of my grandpa, Addy. When you first came here. He was just as high-spirited. Did I tell you he lived with the Choctaw too?"

"What happened to him?"

"He ran off."

Mr. Frank's ma clears her throat, says, "Now, Frank . . ." but Mr. Frank stops her.

"He was selfish, Ma. You and me both know that. He didn't think of anyone but himself. Not like Addy. You know about helping others, Addy. You bring cures."

Mr. Frank, he's serious. Even the doctor stops chewing for a minute to have a good, long look at me.

"I sure do admire you, and I don't wish you were anywhere else but here," Mr. Frank says.

Dr. Hill says he will train me to become a midwife to help birth babies, and in the meantime, I teach myself the multiplication tables, for I hope to make substantial gains in a financial way. Word gets out about my curing Thelma Addy's thrush, and soon enough people are bringing their babies over from Jasper, Simpson, and Rankin counties, from far and near, so I may make them the tea, breathe on them, and exert my powers in curing them of thrush.

I know about building schoolhouses. I know about keeping the rain and wind out. I know where to find herbs and roots that can make a good cure. And now? Now I know about helping babies.

Ever since he delivered me to court, Mr. Tempy stepped away and disappeared back into the woods with Zula and the other Choctaws. Until, that is, they come by to visit. I go rushing down from the porch toward the road when I see them. I run to Zula. I tell her everything about little Thelma Addy and all the other babies I've helped.

We hold and hug each other. Her cheeks are honey gold from laughing. I introduce Little Bit. I say, "See this woman? She's an angel." Then I tell Zula, "See this girl? She's my best friend."

Zula laughs and says she can see this girl, Little Bit, and she has seen her before.

"I see you two fighting by the creek long ago. And you see now? Now you are friends. All of us are friends."

But Zula tells us she and Mr. Tempy are not here to celebrate. They have come by to say their farewells.

It turns out that once the town of Raleigh discovered their settlement, the sheriff and others forced them and all the Choctaw to leave Smith County for good.

"Why can't they just leave you be?" I ask Mr. Tempy.

"They want the land, same as before and same as before that," Mr. Tempy says. "Fighting's mostly about land, money, and women. These people in Mississippi won't ever be satisfied until every single Choctaw is out of here."

I hear Mr. Tempy and Mr. Frank talk over the situation. When white people came into Mississippi, they wanted the Choctaw land, so they made the Choctaw make an agreement at Dancing Rabbit Creek. If any of the Choctaw stayed, they could stay not as Choctaw but as citizens of the state of Mississippi. That was very upsetting to the Choctaw because being a Choctaw to a Choctaw is more important than being a Mississippian.

After the war, the white people around here grumbled not only because they lost, but because they had to be citizens of their enemy—the federal government. Being a citizen of the United States is supposed to be more important than being a Mississippian. Seems like we would know better. Seems like we would understand how to get along with everybody after what all we've been through.

"We have to leave our country," Zula says. "Grief has made children of us. Many winters ago our chiefs sold our country. Every warrior opposed the treaty. Our land was taken away. We do not now complain. The Choctaw suffers, but he never weeps."

Mr. Frank loads them up with a heap of supplies from the store. They saddle their horses, and before they ride off, Zula calls to me.

"Chahta hapia hoke," she says.

"What does that mean?" Little Bit says.

"We are Choctaw," I say, waving goodbye to them all.

One day, midsummer, Garner comes by the store for supplies. He tells us news that both Mr. Smith and my pappy have been pardoned by the new governor of Mississippi, a governor who was elected to the legislature and fought for white supremacy right alongside Pappy as a member of the Ku Klux Klan. Now that Pappy is out, Garner says he's moving so Pappy can't find him.

"You have to do what you can do, then move on and do some more," Mr. Frank says.

"He plowed me once and once was enough," Garner says.

Mr. Frank outfits Garner and only charges him half.

They have themselves a farewell. They rub each other's backs and say to each other, "Stay safe."

We find out about Pappy from others who visit Mr. Frank's store. Soon as Pappy got out, Pappy went after Smasher, of all people. Right after church, they got to drinking down by the creek where their horses drank and Pappy pulled on Smasher's new mustache. The knives came out and Smasher cut across Pappy's stomach. It is said that his entrails fell out and that Pappy knelt there in the creek, washed them, and stuffed them back inside himself. Smasher himself bound him up around the stomach with his shirt, then rode him to someone who sewed him up. And not long afterward, that very evening, we hear that Pappy climbed on a stump and crowed like a rooster, amazed to be alive.

I never once hear from anybody about Momma or what happened to her or where she went to in Texas. I like to think that the man with the mule from Mr. Frank and Miss Irene's wedding took Momma all the way to exactly where she wanted to be in Texas. I like to imagine that the man with the mule took care of Momma, fed her, kept her out of the rain and trouble, fixed her a cup of life-everlasting tea. Maybe he even helped her look for my pappy. But after a while, they maybe saw that they had more than Texas in common. After a while, maybe they even fell in love and he decided that a woman like my momma needed just the kind of man he was. A good man to take care of her. Always.

When I think on Momma this way, when I imagine her safe and happy, the angry thoughts leave me alone.

My momma and pappy are no longer the center of my life. I have other things to consider.

The population in Smith County has grown twofold and already they are planning to rebuild the courthouse with updates like a third story and a bell tower. The Tyler Tap Railroad running to the Texas and Pacific Railway is under way too.

I know one thing for sure. I never want to go to Texas.

When people stop by the store, I like to sit on the front porch and read from the Jackson paper out loud for the older ones and the younger ones who cannot read. I tell them news from all over. I read to folks about how they have a place called a "zoo" in Philadelphia, Pennsylvania, where they keep animals just so folks can look. I read to them about the presidential elections too.

Rutherford Hayes runs against Samuel Tilden for the presidency and the final vote is so close, Congress appoints the

Electoral Commission. There is a long period when none of us knows who will lead. We cannot help but comment that sometimes there's not much order, not in No-Bob, not in Smith County, sometimes not even in these new United States.

Days before Ulysses S. Grant's term expires, we find out that Rutherford Hayes is declared the winner of the election, and he is inaugurated as our nineteenth president. Some call it "The Great Swap" because they say Hayes got the presidency in exchange for some sort of promise.

We don't pay much mind to Hayes or to the rest of the country.

One day I am on Mr. Frank's store's front porch reading about the Old Confederates' Reunion, where two old Confederates got into a fight with their forks. Mr. Frank, Mr. Frank's ma, and I, we are laughing just to think of those two old soldiers when we see Sunny Rise walking up the road, strong and healthy, with his wife, Early Rise, their friend Please Cook, and her son Deuteronomy.

Sunny takes his hat off to greet us, then tells us all about the store on the Taylorsville-Williamsburg road with the coffeepot hanging over the door. Garner O'Donnell owns it now. Not too long ago a customer found his coffee too hot and said, "Mister, this is hot coffee." Garner liked that and said,

"Mister, this *is* hot coffee." And that's the name of the town now. Hot Coffee.

"Now, isn't that something?" Mr. Frank's ma says. "That Garner started a store, then named a town."

Sunny says he and his family, Please Cook, and Deuteronomy are moving on and they are here to buy, but Mr. Frank won't let them pay and we load them up with supplies. They are on their way toward Hot Coffee to settle on the highest point in Covington County, on a ridge called Hopewell.

Mr. Frank takes care of the steady and ever-increasing traffic of men setting up the sawmills, for there are so many mills popping up in these parts, and so much felling and sawing and chopping, that soon there won't be but a few of these fine longleaf pines left. What with the rails and all the sawmills, there won't be much wilderness left to run to either, for there are fewer woods and fewer and fewer deer and wild turkey roaming.

By the end of the summer, Mr. Frank's store is such a success he has to go to the market in New Orleans to trade and get more supplies sooner than he had planned. I mark off days on the storekeeper's calendar until he comes home safe.

Not but two weeks after Mr. Frank left, he returns, unharmed and unrobbed. He's brimming with supplies and stories of the city. He has with him a brand-new, cast-iron cookstove. The Davenports and other neighbors come to look and inspect as Mr. Frank sets it up. There is the smallest of chills in the air, and when Mr. Frank lights the stove, we gather round to warm our hands. We all marvel at the cookstove's efficiency. Before, all we had was a fireplace, a long-handled skillet, a coffee kettle, a coffeepot, and a coffee mill. Mr. Frank tells me and Little Bit how the cookstove will change everything about our way of life.

Mr. Frank talks up his idea of bringing big items such as the cookstove to the store so other people in Smith County can have such things. He considers taking out a peddling license for a two-horse wagon and traveling all over the county.

"Better times coming," Brother Davenport sings out.

"I'm so glad the younger ones won't have to go through the cruel, hard times we've had," Mr. Frank's ma says, holding her grandbaby and namesake.

"Best thing about all of our troubles is that they taught us to be kind and loving to our enemies," Brother Davenport says. "Taught us to work hard and pray to the good Lord. Then we can do most anything that we wish to do."

And it's true that that little baby Thelma Addy will have it easier, what with cookstoves and such. Manufacturing like this is springing up all over the country, causing us all to reconsider ourselves and maybe start to lay the old things aside.

But there is something to be said for hardships and hard living too.

Mr. Frank tells us all about everything he has learned. He tells us about a new game called "tennis" and a gadget that lets you speak with people across town or even across county lines. They have a building ten stories high in Chicago that people say scrapes the sky. And then there is the sewing machine so that Miss Irene and I can make our garments with less labor.

We all look at the new cookstove and at one another and know that we are living in a world of great conveniences. But I can't help but wonder, *Will this make us good people? Better people? Or will this make us weaker?* I can't rightly tell. I wonder when the feeling of possibilities ends. Who knows what the future will bring. But right now? Right now we are just warming up.

"Thank you for minding the store and everything else, Addy," Mr. Frank says.

I am so full up with warmth and happiness that I have to excuse myself and go to the schoolhouse, where I have myself another look at the geography maps Mr. Frank keeps there. On top of my old desk, I roll out the map of Mississippi.

Living with Mr. Frank and Miss Irene and now Miss Thelma Addy has set my mind on the future and finding my own place. I know a lot about helping. I help run a store and a farm and a family. I helped testify against my own father in a trial that decided his fate, a trial that gave Jess Still Rise his due, bringing a kind of justice here that I had not thought possible. I know how I am like and how I am not like Momma and Pappy and the other O'Donnells of No-Bob, Mississippi. And I know that just because I was born into badness doesn't mean I have to live with it forever.

I wonder and worry about Rew Smith and how when he grows up, will he fret about having been a little part of his pappy's undoing? Or will he just be relieved that Sunny Rise got away?

I can remember clearly the day Mr. Frank showed us schoolchildren this map of the country. And today I see the world all charted out and made right again. From where I stand, the states and the borders look so clear.

I put my finger on where I know No-Bob is. Bob couldn't get out of No-Bob, but I did.

I move my finger a few inches up and down on the map.

I've been to Jasper County and to Jones. I've seen a good part of this world now. What will I do next? Maybe I'll marry and stay here in these few bits that make up Smith County. Or maybe I'll find some other fellow in Simpson or Rankin County. Or maybe I will go and take the Three Notch Road and head out by myself across the Alabama River to Mobile, or go the other way toward Natchez. Or maybe I will just find me a river and follow it to its source.

Author's Note

I began writing *When I Crossed No-Bob* in my parents' home in Pass Christian, Mississippi, a Gulf Coast town of about 6,500 before Hurricane Katrina hit.

This yellow house built in 1845 meant a great deal to my family. It was my parents' dream, their summer home meant to make up for a lot of other lost homes. During World War II, my mother lost her childhood home in Vienna, Austria. More recently, my father lost his childhood home in Newton, Mississippi.

My husband and I got married at the house in Pass Christian; our son learned how to walk on the beach out front; our family spent most every holiday there together; we brought friends there for vacations; and I wrote many stories, essays, and books there.

Katrina took its toll on Pass Christian. Ninety percent of the buildings were leveled. Most of the town's people were left homeless.

Our house is there and it is not. It is a shell with very few walls. It is still standing, but just barely. The destruction is breathtaking. The reconstruction is slow and ongoing.

When I finally settled down to write *When I Crossed No-Bob,* I couldn't help but think I was writing about more than one reconstruction in Mississippi.

I come from a family of war survivors—on both sides. My mother survived Nazi-occupied Vienna, Austria. A good many of my father's people lived through the Civil War. At this writing, the United States is in its fourth year of warring in the Middle East.

Whereas *How I Found the Strong* was based on the real life of one of my relatives, Frank Russell, *When I Crossed No-Bob* is Addy's story. Abandoned by her parents, Addy is a survivor, a young girl living through a difficult situation during one of the worst times in the South's history.

I know that when put to the test, people, young and old, can do tremendous things. Average people transform into noble, strong, resilient human beings—perhaps the very human beings they were meant to become. This was my hope for Addy.

As I neared completion of Addy's story, my father told me about a girl some of his relatives took in after she had fallen on hard times. The couple grew to love this girl and adopted her, raising her as their own. My father referred to this girl as his cousin, who, he says, worked and studied hard, then grew up to become a nurse.

At this writing, the people of Pass Christian are still living in FEMA trailers and tents. I keep hearing a need to get back to "normal." But I have to admit, I want more and better than normal for Mississippi.

It is wonderful to complete a novel, but it is sad too, because to finish means that you have to say goodbye to all the characters, people whom you've come to see as your friends and family now, people you have come to know and love so well. You've lived with them and dreamed about them.

You've worried about them. So when I began *When I Crossed No-Bob,* I was both excited and relieved to return to the Smith County in my imagination, if only to check back in on the Russells and Frank. Still, it's hard to say goodbye to them a second time.

Acknowledgments

My thanks to the University of Evansville for granting me a sabbatical leave so that I could research and write, to the Mississippi Association of Arts & Letters, to the Indiana Library Association and the Mississippi Library Association for inspiring me to continue to write about Frank Russell and Mississippi. And thank you too to my father, James McMullan, and Mr. Gene Tullos of Raleigh, Mississippi, who both took the time to tell me more and more about Smith County. Thanks to Maureen Duncan for all of her help. Thanks to my sister, Carlette McMullan, and my brother-in-law, John Gibbons, who brought Madeleine Honor Gibbons into the world so that I could dedicate this book to her. Thanks too to my mother, Madeleine, who always takes the time to listen. I could not have written this book without my husband, Pat O'Connor, our friends, their children, our son, James, his friends, and all the schoolchildren I've corresponded with and visited. And many, many thanks must go to my agent, Jennie Dunham, manuscript editor, Susan Buckheit, and Margaret Raymo of Houghton Mifflin, who said the magic words, "What's next?"

Margaret McMullan is the author of *How I Found the Strong,* which *Kirkus Reviews* called "unforgettable" in a starred review. She is a professor and chair of the English department at the University of Evansville, in Evansville, Indiana, where she lives with her husband and son. Her newest book for Houghton Mifflin Harcourt is *Cashay.*

New from the author of *When I Crossed No-Bob:*

In her fourteen years living in a Chicago housing project, Cashay has never ridden in a taxi cab, seen the city lit up at night, or set foot in a museum. She's not pretty, or graceful, or bubbly like her little sister, Sashay. She gets her family by on a couple of dollars and food stamps every week.

No, Cashay has never felt much like a treasure. "Your name doesn't signify who you are," Cashay tells her sister.

But that was before Sashay was killed. Before her mother started using again. Before her mentor, Allison, showed Cashay a bigger piece of the world and encouraged her to finally, finally step into it.

A name may not signify who you are, but in this poignant coming-of-age story by the acclaimed writer Margaret McMullan, readers will find that indeed, *Cashay* is an exception to her own rule.

The first novel for young readers by the author of *When I Crossed No-Bob:*

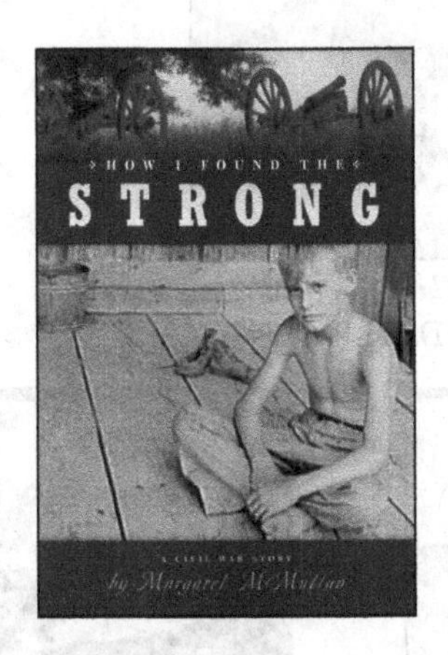

It is the spring of 1861, and the serenity of Smith County, Mississippi, has been shattered by Abraham Lincoln's declaration of war on the South. Young and old are taking up arms and marching off to war. But not ten-year-old Frank Russell.

Although he is eager to enlist in the Confederate army, he is not allowed. He is too young, too skinny, too weak. After all, he's just "Shanks," the baby of the Russell family. War has a way of taking things away from a person, mercilessly. And this war has taken a lot from Frank. It's nabbed his Pa and older brother. It's stolen his grandfather, his grandmother. It's robbed Frank of a simpler way of life, food, his boyhood. And gone are his idealistic dreams of heroic battles and hard-fought victories.

Now all that replaces those images are questions: *Will I ever see my father and brother again? Why are we fighting this war? Are we fighting for the wrong reasons? Will things ever be the same around here?*

★"Unforgettable." —*Kirkus Reviews,* starred review

Enjoy more historical fiction!

The Bronze Bow
by Elizabeth George Speare

Thin Wood Walls
by David Patneaude

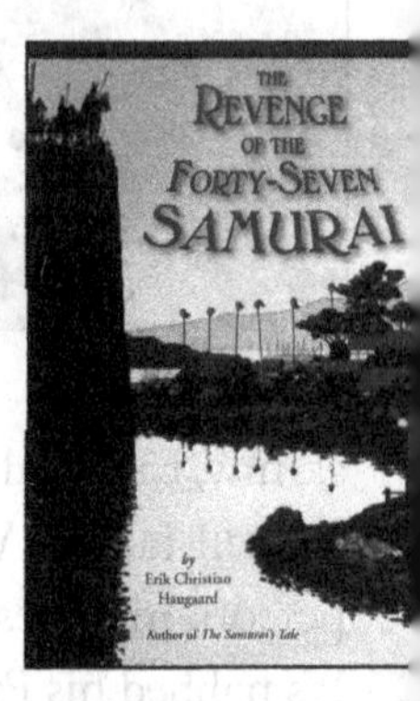

The Samurai's Tale, The Boy and the Samurai, and *The Revenge of the Forty-seven Samurai*
by Erik Christian Haugaard

The Fire-Raiser
by Maurice Gee

Abe Lincoln Grows Up
by Carl Sandburg

More strong heroines!

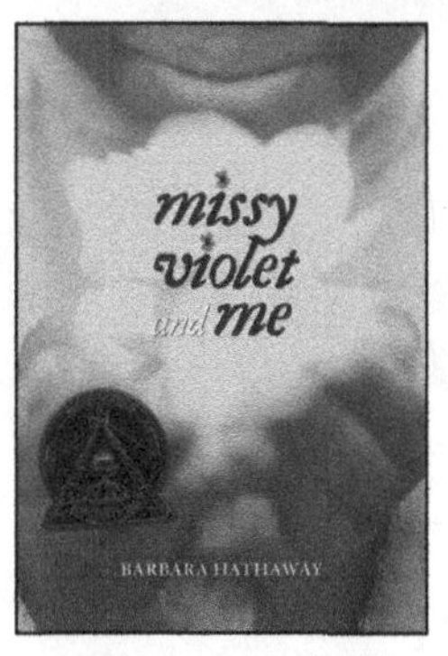

Missy Violet and Me
by Barbara Hathaway

A Coming Evil
by Vivian Vande Velde

Bread and Roses, Too
by Katherine Paterson

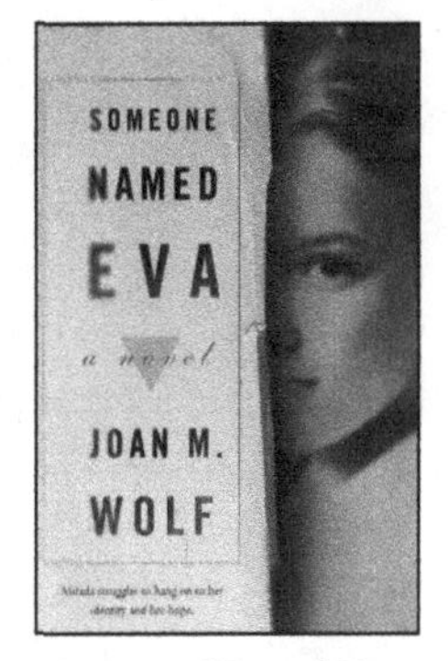

Someone Named Eva
by Joan M. Wolf

The Bread Winner
by Arvella Whitmore

Echoes of the White Giraffe and *Gathering of Pearls*
by Sook Nyul Choi